A Wonderful Adventure

Part Six

The Brilliant Secret

Prometheus

Published by
Chipmunkapublishing
United Kingdom

http://www.chipmunkapublishing.com

Copyright © Prometheus 2025

ISBN   978-1-78382-7411

Dedication

I want to thank May, who excelled in creating the cover for *A Wonderful Adventure*. He took a loose idea and transformed it into something beyond my expectations. Below, in his own words, is a bit about him:

Hi, I'm May, and I believe in the power of creativity. I began my drawing journey on Sunday mornings, inspired by the vibrant world of cartoon television, comics, and games that captivated me as a child. Drawing quickly evolved from a pastime into a lifelong passion that I carry with me every day.

I am currently studying graphic design at an art university, where I have honed my skills and solidified my ambition to become an illustrator. With each passing year, my dream of owning a studio grew stronger, inspiring me to turn my vision into reality.

Every artist starts somewhere, and I am all too familiar with the struggles that come along the way. I began juggling multiple projects alone until my growing clientele clarified that I needed a team. After much anticipation, I finally launched Kabita Studios, a hub designed to foster professional opportunities for illustrators facing the challenges of unstable income.

My mission extends beyond personal ambition; I aim to reduce unemployment, provide pathways for emerging artists, and elevate our creative industry to compete globally.

At Kabita Studios, we are not just a team; we are a community committed to supporting each other and nurturing our creative talents. I have worked on diverse projects, including children's illustrations, novels, comics, portrait paintings, game assets, emoticons, mascots, and advertising storyboards. While Kabita Studios is still in its early stages, I am optimistic about our growth and what we can achieve together for the future of illustration. Join us on this exciting journey!

Prometheus

Jonny's incredible adventures continue at a rip-roaring, nonstop pace as he is first accused of destroying a young footballer's career by giving him a floppy leg, and the incredible repercussions of what happens when he is sent home on a stretcher. Jonny has to return to face the Icelandic Yule Lads once more in one last nail-biting standoff. Then, without taking time to breathe, Jonny is whisked away to Dark Shadow, the most enormous land mass in the multiverse, in a spaceship that can fly at one thousand times the speed of light to find the Elixir of Light. This is no easy task as it's buried beneath a one-thousand-mile-deep lake made entirely of mercury and hidden in the safest, safest places inside a machine called the Hypericosahedron, in typical Jonny Plumb fashion.

Prometheus

CHAPTER ONE:
THE RETURN

'Who's coming with us to Iceland, Dad?' Jonny asked as they slowly drove back home through the leafy lanes of Rutland.

'Well, son, we did invite Isobel's parents, but her Mother is still as mad as an orangutan in a tight-fitting dress and, luckily, still confined to quarters. Lord Taylor? Well, he has the loathsome task of having to look after her. Charlie can't come, but Nanny Carole, Professor Ziad, and his delicate little parping wife can. Then there's your Mother, Eddie, Legend, Legion and myself, oh and, of course, Isobel.'

Pc Floppy was waiting by the front door as they drove to their home through the wrought iron gates, sweating profusely.

'Yes, Pc Floppy, how can we help?' Sir Ranulf asked as he climbed out of the driver's seat and then began removing the bags of groceries and gifts from the Jungle Queen.

'There's been a complaint, a complaint about Jonny.'

'By who?' Sir Ranulf asked.

'The manager informed me of the Monkey Mayhem Marauders football team. It seems Jonny gave one of his players a floppy leg, but in his excitement, Jonny forgot to unfloppy his floppy leg.'

'Whoops,' Jonny replied, smiling.

'Well, it gets worse, I'm afraid, because, according to the rules, Jonny used an unfair advantage. Jonny has been given a three-match ban, plus, there has to be a replay, to be played at their ground, on a date both teams can agree on.'

'I suppose you're going to tell us that using a ghost is also illegal?' Jonny asked angrily.

'What ghost?' Pc Floppy asked, 'You can't use a ghost. Ghost! What, what, do you mean ghost? Ghosts can't play football, it's not allowed.' Pc Floppy responded with real fear in his voice.

'Jonny was just joking; ghosts can't play football. As for the floppy leg, let's sort that out now.'

'Too late, he is taking legal action against you.'

'What, for a mild dose of floppy leg? I don't believe it.' Sir Ranulf barked.

'He had to be carried into his home on a stretcher. When his wife saw him, she fainted and squashed the cat; the cat ran away and hit a paraffin lamp. The paraffin lamp fell over onto the curtains, and the curtains caught fire and then set the house alight. The fire brigade was called and put out the fire. Still, everything they owned was ruined, plus the cat won't come home. The house got burnt down by a paraffin lamp that it knocked over after it was squashed by its owner, who fainted after seeing her husband being carried into her home on a stretcher and all because Jonny gave the guy, who was playing football, a floppy leg.' Pc Floppy said in one mouthful.

'Whoops,' Legend said sniggering.

'So, what can I do?' Jonny asked meekly.

'It gets worse; you know the wife fainted when she saw her husband being carried into her home on a stretcher and squashed the cat, who knocked over the paraffin lamp that set light to the curtains which burnt down the house, that the firemen put out ruining everything and all their possessions? Well, they weren't insured.'

'Double whoops,' Legion said, giggling.

'So, what can I do?' Jonny asked again.

'Well, it gets worse, you know the wife fainted when she saw her husband being carried into her home on a stretcher and squashed the cat, who knocked over the paraffin lamp that set light to the curtains which burnt down the house, that the firemen put out ruining everything and all their possessions, and the house wasn't insured? Well, neither was the cat, a rare only one of its kind, a pure bread Persian cat, the only one left in the world, never returned.'

'Perhaps they also had a goldfish who could sing Rule Britannia while playing the banjo with its teeth,' Lady Kathleen growled, standing by the front door, seething with the stupidity of Pc Floppy.

'Yes, a pink, tutu-wearing, tap-dancing goldfish,' Jonny said, giggling.

'How on earth did you know that?' Pc Floppy asked, scratching his head.

'Pc Floppy, you are without doubt the dullest cretin that I have ever met. Go away and never darken my door again,' Lady Kathleen said, slamming the front door shut. She added, 'Jonny, find Floppy Leg, the footballer and give him a floppy head.'

'On my way!' Jonny shouted as he, Legend, Legion, and Sir Ranulf jumped back into the Jungle Queen, which went "Chug Bang Parp, Chug Bang Parp" as it trundled down the road.

'Cor, what an old banger! My gran's dead cat can walk faster than that old heap,' Floppy Leg said, not yet realising that Jonny was hiding in the back with Legend and Legion. Sir Ranulf jumped out of the Jungle Queen and purposefully marched over to where Floppy Leg was sitting.

'So, what's this about you wanting to make a...' Sir Ranulf barked, not finishing his sentence on purpose, knowing this loud-mouthed yob would have plenty to say.

'What's it got to do with you, old man?' the floppy yob asked, chewing gum. 'My Dad's got a Jaguar, beat that old heap any day. It will beat anything you own.'

'Really? Would you like to wager a bet on that, you think, knuckle-dragging moron?' Sir Ranulf replied.

'Yeah, you bet. When and where?'

'Are you asking me when you can read or where you left your bra and knickers?'

'Hello, do you remember me?' Jonny asked as he, Legend, and Legion silently crept up behind Floppy Leg, making him jump out of his skin.

'How's the leg now? Any better? Thanks to you, I've been banned for three matches, but I don't think you'll win just because I'm not playing. Far from it, and as for a race! You've already lost that and the football game.'

Jonny, Legend, and Legion leapt back into the Jungle Queen and slowly drove off down the road as the poor old girl spluttered, "Chug Bang Parp, Chug Bang Parp," leaving Floppy Leg to his floppy-leg life.

'Don't you think you should unfloppy floppy legs, Legs?' Sir Ranulf asked, smiling.

'No,' Jonny replied, adding, 'he is one of their best players.'

'Was,' Legend replied, smirking.

* * * * * * *

The Silver Flying Arrow landed silently just a few hundred feet from the massive Skogafoss Waterfall. There, waiting in all his glory, was Gentle Storm.

'Good grief,' Philomena Flatulent Fudge-Bucket said as she first laid eyes on the man-mountain next to the waterfall.

'Well, if you think he's big, wait until you meet Stump Grinding, and if you thought Stump Grinding was big, just wait until you meet Sally,' Jonny said, smiling as he helped everybody climb out of the Silver Arrow Space Ship.

'Jonny, my back,' Isobel screamed as she jumped out of the Silver Arrow Space Ship.

'What's the matter?' Jonny asked.

'I don't know, just searing pain, like someone just stuck a...'

'Pen up your nose,' Jonny interrupted, laughing.

'No, you imbecile, like someone stuck a...'

'Five pens up both nostrils and then wrote their names on a sticky bogie.'

'It's not funny, Jonny, this hurts,' Isobel replied angrily.

'Well, there's not much we can do here, but when we get back home, let's go and see the back specialist and then a nose specialist to remove all the pens.'

Isobel stood up and, although in quite a bit of pain, soon joined the others, who, in stunned silence, stared at the huge waterfall and the vast man-mountain called Gentle Storm.

'Gentle Storm, these are my family and friends,' Jonny shouted at the top of his voice.

'Great name,' Professor Ziad shouted.

'No, he's Icelandic, not a Great Dane,' Jonny shouted back.

'Who's got a Great Dane? I like Great Danes,' Philomena Flatulent Fudge-Bucket yelled back as the spray from the mighty Skogafoss soaked everyone.

'This way,' Jonny shouted as he led Isobel, Sir Ranulf, Lady Kathleen, Eddie Rockhard, Philomena Flatulent Fudge-Bucket, and Professor Ziad towards the small opening where Jonny first disappeared into the darkness, which was now bathed in a gentle light.

'How's the back?' Jonny asked Isobel.

'Warm.'

'What do you mean, warm?'

'As in warm, you know, Jonny, between hot and cold.'

'Yes, very funny.'

'It seems to be getting hot now and more uncomfortable.' Isobel stopped and then suddenly bent over in agony.

'I have to get her away from here,' Jonny said frantically.

'But we have only just got here,' Isobel moaned.

'Well, can you wait for an hour?'

'I have something to help ease her pain,' the Queen of Iceland purred. Sir Ranulf, Eddie, and

Professor Ziad stood in stunned silence as the Queen of Iceland glided in, the soft light bathing her incredible beauty. She gently held Isobel's tiny hand and walked her back towards her Queendom. Sir Ranulf, Eddie, and Professor Ziad didn't move, still gaping in lovestruck awe at the unparalleled beauty of the Queen of Iceland.

'Are you boys just going to stand there dribbling?' Lady Kathleen asked angrily.

'Yes, probably,' Professor Ziad whispered.

'Here, drink this. It will make you feel drowsy at first, but the pain will go in a few seconds,' Queen Amaranta purred as she passed Isobel a glass goblet with a bright green liquid.

'Liquidised frog?' Legend said, laughing. Isobel started to giggle and giggle and giggle.

'Don't worry; it does this to begin with. She might start seeing strange things, but it's fine,' Queen Amaranta said gently and then added, 'Jonny, introduce me to your family.'

'Ok, erm, well, this is my Dad. Dad, this is the Queen of Iceland, who is called Queen Amaranta.'

There was silence. Sir Ranulf was left speechless for the first time in his life. He just stood with a silly, boyish look and a glazed expression.

'Well, aren't you going to say hello?' Lady Kathleen asked as she kicked Sir Ranulf in the shins, causing her more pain than him.

'Err, yes, erm, yes, erm hello, yes, erm, how are you, erm, nice weather we're having,' Sir Ranulf muttered while turning beetroot red, with a ridiculous puppy-eyed look on his face.

'Hello, Queen Amaranta. My name is Kathleen, but you can call me Kathie; all my close friends do. I'm sorry; I honestly don't know what happened to him. A tough, no-nonsense and hard-as-five-brick-walls, but the second he claps eyes on you, he turns to jelly. Look at him, I mean, look at him; he's about as wet as a wet flannel that's all wet.'

'Ok, ok, Mum,' Jonny said, trying to shut his mother up. Now it was Eddie's turn to introduce himself to Queen Amaranta, and just like Sir Ranulf, he stood with his mouth slightly open, with a stupid look on his face, unable to speak. Suddenly, he got a nasty case of jelly leg, where he failed to have any control over his legs whatsoever as they wobbled and wobbled, leaving him walking around like he was drunk.

Professor Ziad walked purposefully over to Queen Amaranta, full of bravado and like Sir Ranulf and Eddie Rockhard before him, his eyes glazed over, his mouth fell wide open, and all he could do was coo like a pigeon. He then proceeded to cluck and wave his arms up and down like a chicken. 'Coo, coo, cluck, cluck, clickety cluck, coo, coo,' he said while he ran up and down. Then Philomena Flatulent Fudge-Bucket got a bad case of wind and started to parp very, very loudly.

'Oh god, I'm so sorry,' Jonny said to Queen Amaranta, almost in tears. 'Perhaps we should come another time when my family are, well, erm, less mad and Professor Ziad has stopped clucking, his wife stopped parping, Eddie's jelly leg gets better, my Dad's stopped drooling, and Isobel has stopped giggling.'

'It is fine, Jonny,' Queen Amaranta managed to say while laughing her head off.

'Whenever you and your wonderfully funny family can return, it will be a joy to meet them again.'

Jonny grabbed the clucking, cooing Professor and wobble-legged Eddie Rockhard by their hands, leading them to the Silver Arrow like he was taking two baby chimpanzees to a tea party. Sir Ranulf hadn't moved and still had a stupid glazed look on his face while Philomena continued to destroy not only the pure air of Iceland but also the Ozone layer as she rattled off parp after parp like a machine gun, or machine bum in her case.

* * * * * * *

'We will have to send you for a CT scan, Isobel,' Doctor Chris 'Porker' Bacon said as he finished his check-up.

'What is a CT scan, Doctor Bacon?' Isobel asked.

'Well, it means Computerised Axial Tomography. You know what an X-ray is, don't you? Well, a CT scan is several X-rays taken all at once from different directions.'

'What do you think, Jonny?' Isobel asked. Jonny couldn't reply because he was doubled up on the floor in hysterics. He tried to repeat the Doctor's stupid name but couldn't because he laughed too much.

'I'm sorry about my son, Doctor, but I think something is wrong with him. Well, I think there is something seriously wrong with my entire family. My husband has not spoken for two days. Our best friend has a severe case of a wobbling leg.

Professor Ziad has turned into a chicken that thinks it's a pigeon, a chicken. Isobel's mother is as mad as a carrot, and Philomena hasn't stopped breaking wind for the past forty-eight hours. I seem to be the only—well, Jonny, Isobel, and I seem to be the only—normal people left,' Lady Kathleen said, and then looked down at Jonny writhing around the floor in hysterics, still unable to repeat the Doctor's name. 'Erm, make that just Isobel and me,' Lady Kathleen added.

Jonny finally stopped giggling but explained to his exasperated mother what exactly was so funny about the doctor's name.

'Mum, his name is Chris P. Bacon,' Jonny giggled.

'Yes, I know his name, dear,' Lady Kathleen said, suddenly laughing. 'Crispy bacon, I get it, crispy bacon,' and then laughed out loud for what seemed an eternity.

'Bad news, I'm afraid,' a beetroot-red and extremely embarrassed Doctor Chris P. Bacon said as he checked the scans.

'Not changed your name to Smoky, then?' Jonny asked, laughing.

'She seems to have some device attached to her lower spine. I don't think I have ever seen anything like this. The craftsmanship of this work is out of this world, and who on earth inserted the fibre optics?' Doctor Chris P. Bacon said, completely ignoring Jonny's childish humour.

'Well, if I told you, you wouldn't believe me,' Jonny replied.

'Try me.'

'No.'

'Please.'

'No.'

'Pretty please.'

'No.'

'Three Orange Dream Bars, please?' Jonny asked cheekily.

'No, I can't do that.'

'Ok, well, I've suddenly just forgotten.'

'Ok, three Orange Dream Bars coming up.'

'Think you will find five Orange Dream Bars,' Legend added.

'So, while we wait, tell me, who operated on Isobel's spine and attached this incredible device to her spine?' Jonny ignored the question and instead asked the Doctor one.

'What kind of device is it?'

'I'm unsure I should...' But before Doctor Chris P. Bacon could complete his sentence, Jonny jumped up and pressed his index finger into the Doctor's temple.

'... tell you,' the Doctor said, bewildered by what had just happened.

'It's ok, I know what it is,' Jonny whispered.

'What is it?' Isobel asked.

'How could you know what it is?' Doctor Chris P. Bacon asked as his secretary handed him five ice-cold lollies. He then gave one to Lady Kathleen, Isobel, Jonny, and the slobbering Legend and Legion.

'Thank you,' everyone replied in unison.

'Uncanny,' Doctor Chris P. Bacon said, shuddering.

'What is? That the noise Legend and Legion make is the same as Isobel's mother sipping soup?' Lady Kathleen said, laughing.

'No, I'm talking about the artistry. It's futuristic; humans couldn't have made it.'

'No one said it was, Crispy,' Jonny added.

'Ok, ok, so tell me, who on earth or not on earth made that?' Doctor Chris P. Bacon said, pointing at the scan.

'The Icelandic Yule Lads,' Jonny replied.

'The Icelandic Mule what?'

'No, not Icelandic Mule what, Icelandic Yule Lads. Thirteen of them live in Iceland, hence the name Icelandic. Well, there are fifteen of them; all hideously ugly, and all have bizarre habits.'

'Such as?' Doctor Chris P. Bacon interrupted.

'Oh, my favourite is Gattepefur, the doorway sniffer.'

'What does he do?'

'You're not very bright, are you?' Jonny replied dryly.

'Something's ticking,' Legend said unexpectedly.

'He's right, something is ticking,' Legion added.

'What's ticking?' Doctor Chris P. Bacon asked.

'Don't get out much, do you, Doc?' Lady Kathleen sneered.

'Oh yes, I can hear it now,' Jonny said. 'It seems to be coming from...'

'ISOBEL,' Legend, Legion and Jonny all said at once.

'We have to get back to Iceland and pay those insidious creatures a visit,' Jonny said, visibly shaken.

'When you say ticking, Jonny, do you mean as in a clock or something more sinister?' Lady Kathleen said and then mouthed, 'Like a bomb?'

'Can you see a watch in those scans and X-rays?' Jonny asked Doctor Chris P. Bacon.

'No, no watch, just this small black box. Excuse me for five minutes; I must ask for a second opinion.'

'Does your back still hurt?' Jonny asked the now fearful Isobel.

'I'm scared, Jonny,' Isobel replied.

'Ok, we need to go, and we need to go now. It's a shame I don't have the Golden Globe with me. Wait here; I will be back before you can say antidisestablishmentarianism.'

Jonny suddenly vanished into thin air while Legend and Legion tried and failed to pronounce the first few letters of antidisestablishmentarianism.

'Ok, got it. Mum, you go home, and I'll take Isobel back to Iceland.'

Jonny held the Golden Globe by the open window as it suddenly morphed into the Silver Flying Arrow Spaceship just as Doctor Chris P. Bacon walked back in with his friend Doctor Lavour Tory, just in time to witness Jonny jumping out of the window while holding Isobel, swiftly followed by Legend and Legion. Both doctors stood in stunned silence as the Silver Flying Arrow Spaceship turned on its axis and accelerated at phenomenal speed.

'Did you see that, Lady Kathleen? Did you see that?' Doctor Chris P. Bacon shouted in amazement.

'Seen it, been in it, you name it, I've done it,' Lady Kathleen replied as she wafted past the stunned doctors and walked out of the hospital.

* * * * * * *

'What do you mean, the Icelandic Yule lads refuse to help?' Jonny asked.

'Well, I cannot make them do anything they refuse. They are already imprisoned and refusing to eat, but they did say that if you return the runes to them, they will remove the device from Isobel's back,' Queen Amaranta replied.

'But without the runes, I cannot build the machine.'

'They had already thought of that.'

'Why? Why would they do that? I can see no reason.'

'As you're aware, they are extremely bright.'

'Yes, so bright that they are now in prison. Doesn't sound very bright to me.'

'That's what I love about you, Jonny; you are so cute and funny.'

'Ah, you're so cute and funny, Jonny,' Isobel mocked.

'Without their help, Isobel, you would still be in a wheelchair,' Queen Amaranta said to Isobel, who was just a bit, ever so slightly, seething with jealousy.

'Yes, and look what they did?' Isobel responded angrily.

'Would you prefer to be in the wheelchair again?' Jonny asked as he grabbed Isobel's hand to comfort her.

'No, of course not,' Isobel replied.

'Then, I must think of a sly and cunning plan, and quickly, as we don't know how much time we have,' Jonny said and added, 'I won't be held to ransom or blackmailed.'

Jonny thought for a second and then said, 'They won't want to kill themselves, right?'

'Kind of defeats the object,' Legion added.

'Well, then we must go there with Isobel.'

'How's that going to help me?' Isobel whined.

'Because if they don't fix it, they will all die.'

'Yes, and so will I,' Isobel said and began crying.

'Listen, old horse; they WON'T kill themselves, so they must fix it, right?'

'What about making a hologram, a replica of Isobel? I mean, they fooled you with the hologram of me,' Queen Amaranta suggested.

'I was just going to suggest that,' Legend said, smiling.

'Ah well, erm, not exactly fooled us, but close; we knew something was not quite right, and, in any case, they can't operate on a hologram, can they?'

'Jonny, you are one smart kid, so sort something out, and I will get Gentle Storm to take you to where they are imprisoned.' Queen Amaranta said as she vanished into the labyrinth of tunnels.

* * * * * * *

'PAL, can you make a perfect hologram of Isobel?' Jonny asked as Isobel waited patiently with Legend and Legion.

'Yes, of course, I can,' PAL replied.

'I mean one that's so good, the Icelandic Yule Lads won't even notice?'

'Yes, of course I can, why?'

'Can you fix it or make it look like a small device is also attached to Isobel's spine?'

'Yes, of course I can, why?'

'Because they have attached a small device to Isobel's spine, and it's ticking.'

'Well, why didn't you tell me? Ok, get Isobel to lie down, and I will check and see what it is.'

As PAL scanned her back with intelligent light, Isobel lay on the world's most comfortable bed.

'Yeah, it's a bomb, alright, and it's set to explode in about thirty minutes,' PAL said matter-of-factly.

'Good grief,' Jonny said in shock.

'Oh God,' Isobel added.

'Can't you stop it?' Jonny asked.

'Err, no,' PAL replied.

'Ok, then we have to make this hologram good; better than good, it's got to be perfect.'

'Jonny, since when do we barter with morons?' Legend asked.

'Since they attached a ticking device to my girlfriend's spine, and you're right, Legend, I don't want to barter with them at all. I fear we can only beat these guys with stealth and sneakiness.'

'How about brute force first and then some sneakiness?' Legion added.

'Yes, we could do that and lose Isobel, but I prefer to be sneaky rather than aggressive. If sneaky doesn't work, then we shall use brute force. Is that a deal?'

'Ok,' Legend and Legion replied in unison.

'Jonny, I love you, Jonny.'

'Yes, I know that, Isobel.'

'What was that, Jonny? Were you talking to me?'

'Of course, I was silly; you just told me you loved me.'

'No, I didn't.'

'Yes, you did.'

'No, I didn't.'

'Jonny, I would like you to meet Isobel. Isobel, I would like you to meet Jonny,' PAL said as Isobel stood next to Isobel.

'Which one of us is real, Jonny?' Isobel and Isobel asked.

Jonny stood open-mouthed, with that bewildered, dumb, lost child look on his face as he stared intently at both Isobels.

'Well?' both Isobels asked.

'Well, I can't tell,' Legend said as he sniffed both Isobels.

'Nor me,' Legion added.

'That's incredible, PAL, absolutely incredible,' Jonny said as he walked around both Isobels.

'Yes, it is. I have also made exact replicas of the thirteen runes,' PAL replied, trying not to sound in the least bit smug.

'Can they sing?'

'Doh, dim, dumb Jonny, he just told you they were exact replicas so that they can sing. They can sing, can't they PAL?' Legend asked.

'Oh yes, they can sing, just listen, but which ones are real?' Jonny listened to both runes singing and couldn't tell any difference. Then both

Isobel's sang; again, Jonny couldn't tell the difference.

'Right, we must go as we are running out of time,' Jonny said as he grabbed the wrong Isobel by the hand.

'Ahem,' Isobel said.

'Oops, best I take the right Isobel,' Jonny said nervously.

'No, you must take both. Now, this is the plan. You walk in with the real Isobel as they need to remove the bomb, but there will be a standoff. Please do not give them the runes until the bomb is removed or the ticking stops. When it does, I will play a few tricks with them, swap the hologram Isobel with the real Isobel, and get back here ASAP, ok?'

'Ok,' Jonny replied.

Hologram Isobel disappeared as Legend ran off to get Stump Grinding and Sally in case they needed extra muscle.

* * * * * * *

Gentle Storm pushed the sizeable wooden cell door open. The smell was unbearable.

'Did you bring the runes?' Gattepefur asked.

'Yes,' Jonny replied.

'Then pass them over to me.'

'No, I will only hand them over to you when you have removed the bomb.'

'No, I will only operate on her when I have the runes,' Gattepefur replied.

'Ok, Gattepefur, then we will all die,' Jonny replied, asking him, 'How much time is left?'

'Five minutes.'

Jonny stood still with Legend and Legion, holding Isobel's hand. Jonny took the bag of runes out of his pocket and held them up in the air.

'Let me see them,' Gattepefur hissed.

'When you begin to operate,' Jonny replied. A small bead of sweat trickled down Gattepefur's ugly face, then another and another. Time was running out, and still, this dangerous game continued.

'Isobel, lie down,' Jonny said gently, then, turning to Gattepefur, said, 'You have two minutes to remove the bomb.'

'And you have two minutes to hand over the runes.'

Tentatively, Jonny handed over the runes, which were hurriedly snatched by Gattepefur, who quickly opened the bag. He smiled, showing off all his bad teeth, and nodded to his Icelandic Yule Lad brothers. Within seconds remaining, they had quickly and painlessly removed the bomb. As quick as a flash, the honest Isobel was replaced with the hologram Isobel, but not just one—one hundred, and each one had a small bomb attached to its spine. They weren't real, of course, but the Icelandic Yule Yobs didn't know that, did they? Gattepefur looked up and then at the one hundred holograms of Isobel and gulped. Jonny, the honest Isobel, Legend, and Legion quickly ran out of the dingy, stinking cell and back towards the Silver Flying Arrow as Gentle Storm slammed the wooden cell door closed and ran.

Jonny counted, '5, 4, 3, 2, and 1.'

'KERBOOOOOM!'

Jonny checked Isobel's open wound.

'Can you fix that, Pal?' He jumped out of the Silver Arrow and headed towards the awaiting Queen Amaranta.

'They're not dead. I wouldn't do that, but they won't wake up anytime soon, and when they do, they will have more and more Isobels to operate on as each one carries the same type of explosion.'

'Which is?' Queen Amaranta asked.

'Oh, nothing much, except for the smelly stink bombs attached to a flash, bang, wallop bomb. That should keep them busy for a few years to come.'

'I'm going to miss you, Jonny.'

'Oh, don't worry, we will be back to visit very soon,' Jonny said as he climbed back into the Silver Arrow Space Ship.

'How often will those stink bombs explode?'

'Oh, every day, each one is fitted with a flash, bang, wallop stink bomb, but if you want more, just ask.'

Queen Amaranta blew Jonny a kiss as the Silver Arrow turned on its axis and was gone in a flash of incredible power.

* * * * * * *

'Isobel will stay with her Auntie Haggis Itchysporan McPlop for a while, Jonny. Because her mother still thinks she is a nine-year-old mountain goat named Ralph. I am unsure if she will ever be allowed home, and as you know, Isobel's father is never around, so therefore can't look after her. We have arranged for her to come and visit in a month,' Lady Kathleen said gently.

'Where is she going to then?' Jonny asked while trying not to cry.

'Scotland,' Lady Kathleen replied, adding, 'but don't fear, you can write and speak to each other on the phone, plus the fresh air will do her some good. After all, she has had quite an experience, hasn't she?'

'Yes, yes, I guess so. When can I see her? I mean, can I see her before she goes?' Jonny asked, almost second-guessing the reply. 'She's gone already, hasn't she?'

'Yes, Jonny, we didn't want to upset you or her further.'

Jonny began giggling softly at first and then louder and louder.

'What on earth is wrong with the boy now?' Sir Ranulf barked as he walked into the kitchen.

'I have no idea,' Lady Kathleen said, noticing Nanny Carole giggling as well. Jonny tried to speak but could not because he had such a bad case of the giggles.

'You know Ranulf, we adopted a star child who can do more than any child in the universe, yet he still acts like a five-year-old.' Lady Kathleen sighed as she looked at Jonny rolling around on the floor, clutching his stomach in fits of laughter.

'When are you going to Dark Shadow, Jonny?' Sir Ranulf asked, but Jonny still had no response.

Five minutes elapsed when Jonny finally stood up, wiping the tears from his face.

'Ahh, that's better,' Jonny said quietly, still chuckling.

'Care to share the joke, son?' Sir Ranulf asked.

'No, it's ok,' Jonny replied as he walked outside to play in the garden while repeating Auntie Haggis Itchysporan McPlop under his breath.

* * * * * * *

'Listen, children, a new date has been set for the rematch against the Monkey Mayhem Marauders,' the new headmistress, Miss Kitkat, announced during assembly.

One single hand shot up into the air.

'Yes, and who may you be?' Miss Kitkat asked as she peered down to the front row of first-form children.

'Gracie, Miss.'

'Hello, Gracie, now what can I do for you?'

'I want to play football instead of Jonny Plumb, Miss.' There was a sudden hushed silence around the assembly hall.

'I'm sorry; did you just say you wanted to play football?'

'Yes, Miss, I did, and I do.'

'But aren't you a bit small and a bit, err, well, girlie to play football in a BOYS' football team?'

'Yes, I am small and a girlie, but where does it say I can't play in a boy's football team?'

'Well, where it says "Boys' Football Team", it's a bit of a giveaway, don't you think, Gracie?'

'No,' Gracie replied matter-of-factly and ever so bravely.

Suddenly, the stunned silence was met with a cacophony of noise as all the schoolchildren chatted.

'Why can't she play, Miss?' Jonny asked.

'In case you didn't hear, because it's a boys' football team.'

'Yes, I heard you, but it doesn't say anything about that in the rules, does it?'

Miss Kitkat turned to Mr. Boil, the sports teacher, and shrugged her shoulders.

'I will have to check, but for a girl to play? It's highly irregular,' Mr Boil replied.

'Ok, quiet school, we will now sing "All things bright and beautiful",' Miss Kitkat bellowed.

'When's the football match then, Miss?' Jonny asked.

'Oh, this Friday, don't forget we are playing away. Now be upstanding.'

Assembly over, Jonny walked over to where Gracie was, a small, blond-haired girl with a twinkle in her eye.

'I liked what you said,' Jonny said, smiling.

'Thank you, Jonny, you're my hero,' Gracie replied, blushing.

'Erm, well, I guess you can play football then?' Jonny asked.

'Yes, I can play.'

'But aren't you scared? I mean, did you see the last game?'

'Yes, I did; they don't scare me. I may be just a girly, but I have six brothers, so I had to be tough.'

'Ok, well, I will talk to Biffo Brown, and if he agrees and you can play, we will get you to come to the practice matches and training.'

'I won't let you down, Jonny, I promise,' Grace said as she skipped the corridor to her first lesson.

* * * * * * *

'We have to go to Dark Shadow soon,' Jonny said as he sat with Legend and Legion, dangling his feet in the cold water of the little stream in his back garden.

'Are you ok, Jonny?' Legend asked, picking up on Jonny's nervousness.

'I'm unsure.'

'Why?' Legion asked as he watched, mesmerised by Chubb, the friendly goldfish, as it darted up and down the stream with his friends.

'I, I don't know, I just feel...'

'...Scared?' Legend interrupted.

'Yes, very scared.'

'Not surprising, is it? Legion added that this place is undoubtedly the most dangerous in the multiverse.

'Yeah, that makes Jonny more fearful,' Legend added.

Jonny looked at Chubb as he raced up and down, occasionally leaping out of the water while performing a perfect barrel roll and diving back into the water.

'That's the kind of freedom I want,' Jonny murmured.

'Oh, you want to be a goldfish now, Jonny?'

'Part of me does.'

'Which part?' Legend asked.

'His fins,' Legion said, giggling, while not taking his eyes off Chubb and his friends as they raced up and down.

'Like flying underwater,' Jonny said as he watched, almost mesmerised by Chubb's antics.

'So, how are we going to get this elixir thingy, then, Jonny?' Legend asked as he stared into the stream.

'Elixir,' Jonny corrected.

'Yes, that's the thing.'

'Legend, I don't have a clue.'

'Well, we know Jonny's dumb, but what about the elixir thingy?' Legion added, smiling.

'I only have a few days to sort it out.'

'Perhaps you should ask PAL,' Legion added as he began to paw at the water.

'Or Spirit,'

'Or Cosmos,'

The three sat silently, staring into the water, watching Chubb and his friends race up and down. They were so enchanted that they failed to hear Nanny Carole calling them in for tea.

'Jonny, I have been calling you for ages. Now come in and have your tea,' Nanny Carole said in her dark, melted chocolate voice, which still made Jonny's heart skip a beat.

'Are you ok, son, you seem very quiet?' Sir Ranulf asked.

'He's worried about Isobel,' Lady Kathleen said while stroking Jonny's little hand.

'No, I'm worried about going to Dark Shadow,' Jonny replied, twisting his spaghetti around his fork.

'Where's Dark Shadow, Jonny?' Lady Kathleen asked.

'It's further away than you could ever imagine, and it's larger than you could ever imagine, and we have to find something enclosed in a trap which is cleverer than anything you could imagine,' Jonny replied, almost mournfully, and then added, 'and I am scared.'

'Have you spoken with Spirit, Cosmos or even PAL yet?' Sir Ranulf asked as he placed his knife and fork beside his plate, leaving his food uneaten.

'No, not yet, but I will tomorrow or when I go to bed tonight,' Jonny replied, and then remembered about the girl at school who wanted to play in the football team and asked, 'Dad, can a girl play in the school football team?'

'Yes, of course, why not?'

'Erm, because she's a girl and only about ten.'

'Ten? Ten what, inches tall?' Lady Kathleen said, laughing.

'No, Mum, ten years of age, but apparently, she's good at football, and you know I'm not allowed to play.'

'Well, we have training tomorrow as the game is this Friday, isn't it, Jonny?'

'Yes, this Friday.'

'Well, bring her along tomorrow, by which time I will have checked the rules and how to break them,' Sir Ranulf replied, laughing.

'I'm going to bed now,' Jonny said as he stood up and walked out of the kitchen, 'night Mum, night Dad.'

'Night, son, don't worry, everything will be alright. I am sure she will be able to play.'

'I wasn't worried about that, Dad; I am worried about Dark Shadow.'

* * * * * * *

Jonny lay on his bed with his two faithful companions lying on the floor, snoring heavily.

'Help me, Spirit,' Jonny whispered, but there was no reply.

'Help me, Cosmos,' Jonny whispered sadly; there was still no reply.

'Help me, Cheroo,' Jonny whispered again. Still no response. The only noise, apart from the two snoring dogs, was the wind as it moaned and the rustling of the leaves in the back garden.

'I think you are alone, Jonny,' Legend whispered.

'Yes, I think you are right. Oh well, perhaps tomorrow I should speak with PAL.' Jonny pulled Pod up to his chest, closed his eyes and fell fast asleep.

* * * * * * *

'Well, Jonny, your young lady friend can play for the school football team. So, bring her to practice tonight, and we will see how she gets on,' Sir Ranulf said as he neatly folded his napkin.

'Thanks, Dad,' Jonny replied as he picked up his school satchel and headed out the door to catch the rickety old, sick-smelling school bus.

'One half to ...'

'Hello Jonny, did you hear any news about me playing for the football team?' Gracie asked, tugging vigorously at Jonny's sleeve.

'... West House, please.'

'Jonny, did you find out, pleeeeeeeeeeease?' Gracie pleaded, but Jonny seemed to have his mind on other things, such as flying to Dark Shadow.

Jonny smiled and quietly said, 'Practice well tonight, impress the team captain, and I think you will have a great chance of playing.'

'Yippeeeeeeeeeeeeee, I love you, Jonny,' Grace shouted at the top of her voice, and for a small girl, she had one robust set of lungs.

'Will you come and watch, Jonny?' Grace shouted from behind a school bus's noisy, smelly, untidy rust bucket.

'Erm, yes, if I can,' Jonny replied and then stared blankly out of the window as the cacophony of noise rose. Luckily, Jonny could enter into a calm state, which he had learned while he was a student on Planet Boddhi.

* * * * * * *

'Jonny, wake up; something is hovering in the back garden,' Nanny Carole whispered as she shook Jonny's big toe.

'Eh, what's something in the back garden?'

'I don't know, but it's very, very big. Look for yourself if you don't believe me,' Nanny Carole said as she pulled the flimsy curtains open, allowing the sunlight to shine like a billion suns.

Jonny immediately pulled the blankets back over his head, plunging himself into darkness again.

'Jonny, you need to see this,' Legend urged as Legion removed the blanket in one swift move.

'Good God and jumping Jehoshaphat,' Jonny exclaimed as he peered out his window. Still dressed in his striped pyjamas, Jonny ran downstairs, followed by the ever-attentive Legend and Legion.

'Jonny, there's something...'

'... Yes, Dad, I know,' Jonny said, interrupting a very surprised Sir Ranulf.

'Darling, there's something huge...'

'... Yes, Mum, I know,'

'Jonny, there's some...'

'... Yes, Charlie, I know,' Jonny shouted as he ran past a very bewildered Charlie.

Jonny, Legend, and Legion stood stock still and in absolute silence, apart from heavy panting.

'Nice surprise for a Friday morning?' Sir Ranulf said as he nudged Jonny in the back.

'Yeah, I wasn't expecting that,' Jonny replied, smiling.

'Why are you smiling, son?'

'I asked for some help when I went to bed last night. I didn't think anybody heard, so I assumed I wouldn't get any, but to get this, it's just incredible.'

'Why would they send you that?' Sir Ranulf exclaimed.

'Dunno, perhaps to help me get to Dark Shadow.'

'Well, it will certainly do that,' Legend butted in.

'But what is it?' Legion asked as he peered up around this vast machine, which looked a bit like the Silver Flying Arrow but was even more futuristic and sleeker.

'Soon, find out, I guess,' Jonny replied as he walked up to this vast, silent machine that almost filled the entire garden. He held his hand up to touch it, and as soon as he felt it, it appeared to ripple in iridescent colours.

'Hello, Jonny,' the spaceship said in the softest woman's voice he had ever heard.

'He... he... hello,' Jonny replied, embarrassed.

'Jonny, she is beautiful,' Sir Ranulf said, drooling, as he stood in absolute awe. 'I thought my old Spitfire was something and then the Silver Arrow, but this, this is just unbelievable.'

'Jonny, step inside,' the ever so gentle, crushed velvet voice asked.

'But how do I step in?' Jonny asked, looking up, then down and from side to side.

'Just step towards me.' Jonny took two steps forward and suddenly found himself inside an empty, vast, pearl, white room. He turned around and could still see Legend, Legion, Sir Ranulf, Lady Kathleen, Charlie, and Nanny Carole all standing gawking open-mouthed. Jonny waved, but they didn't wave back as they couldn't see him. You could see out, but no one could see in.

'Welcome, Jonny. My name is Rapture, but unlike Pal, I am not the ship's computer.'

'Then, what are you then?'

'I am Rapture.'

'Ok then, if you're not the computer, what are you?'

'I am Rapture.'

'Yes, I remember having a similar conversation with Darkness,' Jonny replied, shaking his head.

'But I am not Darkness. I am the light, and I am called Rapture.'

'Ok, I get the idea, I am light, and I get I am Rapture, but would you mind explaining just a teeny weenie a little bit more.'

'I am Rapture, I am...'

'...Oh, for God's sake, I know you are Rapture,' Jonny interrupted angrily.

'As I was saying before you interrupted me, Jonny...'

'If you say you are Rapture once more, I shall scream,' Jonny said.

'Jonny, be quiet and listen. I am Rapture. I am not a computer; I am a living being. I am a living machine, and I am called Rapture.'

'You're a living, breathing, talking...'

'Yes, and flying,' Rapture interrupted, '...machine, but you're a machine? right?'

'Wrong, as I have no moving parts. I am Rapture, I live, and I exist. I am here to take you to your final destination.'

'PAL could have done that, hold on, what do you mean final destination?'

'PAL cannot find Dark Shadow, and the Silver Arrow Spaceship is far too slow.'

'What do you mean, too slow? It can travel twice the speed of light, the fastest machine in the entire multiverse.'

'I am faster, a lot faster. I am Rapture.'

'But that's not possible,' Jonny thought for a moment and then asked, 'How much faster?'

'Oh, just ten thousand times faster.'

'But that's impossible.'

'No, it is not. I am Rapture.'

'That's more than two billion miles in a second.'

'Yes, Jonny, your maths are excellent; it's two billion, nine hundred and ninety-seven million, five hundred and eighty thousand miles, in an Earth second.'

Jonny stood silently and then said quietly, almost whispering, 'Do we go soon?'

'Yes, in one hour, so you had better prepare.'

'What do I need to bring?'

'Just your immense courage, Jonny.'

'How do I get out, Rapture?'

'Getting out of going to Dark Shadow, or getting out of Rapture?'

'Getting out of Rapture, please; I don't think I can get out of going to Dark Shadow.'

'The same way you got in. You have exactly one hour before we leave.'

Jonny turned and walked straight back through the translucent walls, suddenly standing in the back garden again.

'Took your time,' Legend said.

'What do you mean? I have only been about five minutes.'

'No, you haven't; you have been one hour,' Sir Ranulf replied.

'But that's impossible; I was just talking to Rapture, asking her about the ship. Honestly, I couldn't have been more than five minutes.'

'Rupture? Who on earth is Rupture when Rupture's at home?' Legend asked sarcastically.

'That is, and she is called Rapture, not rupture, you dim dog,' Jonny replied, pointing at the sleek machine still hovering behind him.

'Oh, so who named the spaceship Rapture then?' Legion asked, almost as sarcastically as Legend before.

'Ok, she's not a...'

'She, what do you mean, SHE?' Legend interrupted.

'Ok, be very quiet, and I will explain,'

'Ooh, be very quiet, and I'll explain,' both Legend and Legion replied using silly voices.

'Ok, I won't bother then.' Jonny replied as he brushed past both of them.

'Ooooooooooooh, get her. Jonny, we're just fooling with you,' Legend said, trying not to smirk.

'Ok, well she, as in that,' Jonny said, pointing at Rapture, 'is not a spaceship but a living, breathing being, and this living, breathing being is called Rapture. Now wait for this bit; it can fly at ten thousand times the speed of light. What's the speed of light, Legend?'

'Err, dunno,'

'Legion?'

'Err, dunno as well.'

'Morons.'

'When, when do you go?' Nanny Carole asked hesitantly.

'Oh, very soon, I must go in less than one hour.'

Nanny Carole ran inside with tears streaming down her face, followed by Charlie and Lady Kathleen, who went inside to comfort her.

'Don't worry, old boy, they're all just apprehensive about you,' Sir Ranulf said as he ruffled Jonny's long, sleek black hair, adding, 'How long will it take? How long could it take to travel to Dark Shadow?'

'Well, err, apparently, not that long, you know, with bending space and time.'

'I bent a spoon once,' Legend piped in.

'Yeah, by looking at it,' Legion replied, giggling.

'And can you explain what you'll do when you eventually get to Dark Shadow?' Sir Ranulf asked.

'Sadly, no, Dad, because we have yet to work out how to be solid and air.'

'You lost me there, son.'

'Ok, Dad, to get into this machine at Dark Shadow, I must be invisible, but then, I need to be solid enough to remove the elixir but so quiet I won't be heard. Then, I must become invisible again to get out while being solid enough to carry the elixir out of this vast machine called the Hypericosahedron.'

'Is it dangerous, or shouldn't I ask?'

'Yes, to both.'

'Well, son, nobody knows better than you, but when do you intend to go? And what happens if all does not go to plan?'

'Well, there's a good chance that I might be a bit late for school on Monday.' Jonny replied, laughing nervously.

* * * * * * *

'Legend, Legion, go to the toilet and be ready in thirty minutes,' Jonny shouted as he went indoors to change. He ran up the three flights of stairs, grabbed Pod from the unmade bed, hugged it with all his might, and then carefully placed it back on the pillow. Jonny stood staring at it in silence as a little tear fell out of his eye and slowly rolled down his cheek and dripped onto the wooden floor.

'Wait for me, Pod, I won't be long,' Jonny whispered and walked out.

* * * * * * *

'Ok, are you two ready?' Jonny asked Legend and Legion.

'Yes,' they both replied.

'Did you neatly park your breakfast?' Jonny asked, laughing.

'Not quite, more like a road crash, but yes, we did,' Legend replied.

'OK, then we should go. Bye Dad, bye Mum, bye Nanny Carole, bye Charlie, bye Nanny Noo, bye Stan.'

Everybody turned to see Stan and Nanny Noo floating by the kitchen door. Jonny hugged everyone and waved excitedly towards Nanny Noo, who blew Jonny a kiss. Jonny pretended to catch it and placed it in his chest pocket.

Jonny, Legend and Legion walked towards Rapture and, without turning back, walked straight through the spaceship's walls. In silence, Rapture slowly and effortlessly pointed towards the heavens and vanished in a flash of light.

* * * * * * *

'Goooooooooooooooooood Gaaaaaaaaaaaaaaaawd,' Legend and Legion both shouted as they were catapulted through the sky at an incredible, jaw-dropping, beyond-belief speed.

'Relax, the more you relax, the easier it will become,' Rapture said softly.

'How can we relax squashed like this?' Legend asked as he and Legion were squashed almost flat against the translucent wall.

'Where's Jonny?' Rapture asked. 'Sous vous,' ('under you') Jonny replied, almost unable to breathe, let alone speak.

'What on earth are you talking about?' Legend asked, laughing.

'Je ne me sens pas bien,' ('I don't feel very well') Jonny said as he gently floated, turning ever so slightly green.

'Why are you speaking in strange tongues, Jonny?' Legion asked, trying not to laugh.

'Ce n'est pas étrange, c'est français,' ('it's not strange, it's French').

'Sounds very strange to me,' Legion replied.

'And me,' Legend added.

'Français n'est pas étrange,' ('French is not strange').

'Maybe so, but you certainly are,' Legend giggled.

'Je vole comme un oiseau' ('I am flying like a bird').

'You are one strange fish, Jonny, one strange fish,' Legion added.

'Pourquoi est-ce que je parle en français?' ('Why am I speaking in French?').

'Oh, you're speaking French; we thought there was something insanely bonkers about you,' Legend said, laughing.

'Je pense en anglais, mais le français sort de ma bouche,' ('I am thinking in English but only French comes out of my mouth').

'Not just French, Jonny,' Legend replied, laughing.

'Rapture, où sommes-nous?' ('Where are we, Rapture?')

'We have just passed the sun.'

'What?' Jonny screamed.

'Ah, you have stopped speaking French, have we?'

'I never spoke in French, you strange reptile, Legend.'

'Yes, you did,' Legend, Legion and Rapture all replied together.

'Que?' ('What?')

'You just did it again,' Legend said, laughing.

'Non, je n'ai pas fait.' ('No, I did not)

'Rapture, why is Jonny speaking in French?' Legend asked.

'I am unsure, Legend, it is unusual, but then again, so is Jonny.'

'You can say that again,' Legion said, giggling.

'I am not unusual. Anyway, how did we get to the sun so quickly?'

'Well, I did say I was fast,' Rapture replied gently.

'Yes, but the sun is ninety million miles away.'

'Your sun is correct, but this isn't your sun. Would you care to look?'

'Not our sun?' Legend silently mouthed.

'So, whose sun is it?' Jonny asked as he stared at the humongous ball of light.

'The universe is not owned, Jonny, so no one owns this sun or, for that matter, owns yours. By the way, this sun is ever so slightly bigger than what you describe as your sun.'

'So, Rapture, exactly how much bigger than our sun is it?'

'Okay, see that tiny dot to the right of this sun?'

'Yes,' Legend, Legion and Jonny all replied.

'Well, that's the same size as yours.'

'So, where are we, and why are we where we are?' Jonny asked, frowning.

'Good question, Jonny. To reach Dark Shadow, which is so far away, it's beyond comprehension; we have to align ourselves to a millionth of a Planck length.'

'What?' Jonny said, open-mouthed.

'We have planks in our back garden,' Legend whispered to Legion, who began giggling around the floor.

'You're a pair of planks,' Jonny said, smiling, and then added, 'So, Rapture, what are you talking about?'

'Okay, like I said, we must align ourselves very precisely, and then when we have done that, we can bend time and space. But if we are even half a Planck's length out, we all die.' Jonny gulped and then asked, 'Please explain the size of this erm, Planck.'

'Okay, well, the size of the Planck length can be visualised as follows: if a particle or dot about 0.1 mm in size (which, by the way, is the smallest object the unaided human eye can see) were magnified in size to be as large as the observable universe, then inside that universe-sized dot, the Planck length would be roughly the size of an actual 0.1 mm dot. In other words, a 0.1 mm dot is halfway between the Planck length and the size of the observable universe on an algorithmic scale.'

'Ah, well, glad we cleared that up then,' Legend said, still rolling around the floor in hysterics.

'Yes, I will sleep much better now that I know that', Legion added.

'Yeah, you lost me as well,' Jonny said, smiling.

'Where did you lose me, Jonny?' Rapture asked.

'Oh, right at the beginning.'

'Well, just imagine something so small it would have to be enlarged to the size of the universe to be seen, and it will still be a tiny dot.'

'Like Legend's brain?' Jonny said, laughing. 'Yes, but bigger,' Rapture replied, giggling.

'How long before we get there?'

'We're here.'

'Crikey, that was quick.'

'Well, we have been travelling at ten thousand times the speed of light, so yes, we have been very quick.'

Jonny thought momentarily about travelling at ten thousand times the speed of light. He tried to work out how fast that was in his mind, but words failed him. He mouthed to Legend and Legion, 'ten thousand times the speed of light,' to which they both just shrugged their enormous shoulders.

'Do you know how we can get the elixir, Rapture?' Jonny asked.

'The question is not how, but why?'

'You know, I was thinking about this the other day. Why take something from perfection and give it to fools who will kill to own it? It doesn't make sense, does it?'

'Jonny, your soul is wise, wiser than I thought, and no, it makes no sense. So, ask yourself again, why?'

'I believed I was going to rebuild an ancient alien artefact, but by rebuilding this, I will cause more harm than good, won't I?'

'Good question, Jonny, but in truth, you need to ask yourself a few more questions, such as how long will humanity last, or will it destroy itself from greed? Or if humanity is to last, then we need to help it progress, and by not helping, we then, in fact, start its downfall.'

'Then we must help.'

'Then man will want to own, control, and perhaps sell or, even worse, bring other alien races to earth?'

'Yes, it's the most wanted artefact ever, and whoever owns or controls it has incredible powers.'

'But what if good owned it?'

'Why do you think you have been asked to rebuild it?'

'Ok, so if I rebuild it, no one must know this and have no idea its full potential and power?'

'Correct.'

'But you cannot keep this a secret forever; like I said, many alien races want it, need it and will do anything they can to own it.'

'What if it was made to look like a game or even a ride?' Legend asked. There was absolute silence as Jonny thought about what Legend had just said.

'What's the Disneyland place Dad was talking about, Legend?'

'I am unsure, but I know it's like a theme park in the United States.'

'It is a theme park for children with many exciting rides,' Rapture added.

'So, perhaps we could make it into a new ride, but what exact purpose does it serve?'

'It cures every known sickness in the entire multiverse.'

'Wow, that's going to be a popular ride,' Legion added.

'It also makes people happy.'

'Sorry, what does that mean, Rapture?'

'It means, Jonny, that whoever goes into this machine or ride will instantly be cured of any illness and sickness, plus it automatically makes sad or depressed people happy.'

'Perhaps politicians should use it, and then maybe there could be everlasting peace on earth?'

'Not just on earth, but also in the multiverse, Jonny.'

'But then, every alien race would want to own it for themselves.'

'Back to square one, Jonny,' Legend said ruefully.

'So, then the question is, how do we hide it from them, well, everyone?'

'Well, what about whoever goes into or rides the machine? Is their memory of this machine instantly wiped clean?' Legion asked.

'Wow, you two have suddenly gone up in my estimation,' Jonny said, smiling, adding, 'you know that makes perfect sense, and no one will be any wiser.'

'Hidden in plain sight,' Rapture added.

'Well, ok, then that's sorted. Now all we have to do is find it, bring it home, and build it.' Jonny said with just a slight touch of sarcasm.

'Then we had better get ready to bend time and space. We are nearing the exact spot where we need to be. Just give me a few moments to ensure we are in the right place, and then hold on.' Rapture gently purred.

'Hang on to what?' Jonny asked, wondering if he was about to get squashed again.

'Just relax and float.'

'Is that it, just relax and float?'

'Pretty much, Jonny.'

'Also, how or what is the best way to retrieve the elixir of life from the Hypericosahedron?'

'Now that's going to be very tricky, Jonny. I will tell you when we reach Dark Shadow. Right, we are in position. Are you ready?'

'Err, I guess so,' Jonny replied.

'Legend, Legion, are you ready?'

'Ready,' they both replied.

'Right, before we go, Jonny, I cannot guarantee this will work; if it doesn't, you may all be trapped in space for eternity.'

'Oh, no pressure there then,' Jonny replied, smiling.

'Well, as long as we're not trapped with Jonny speaking French, we don't care, do we Legion?'

'Yes, I do care. I want to go home and grow old gracefully and not stuck in the middle of time and space with a fleabag and a French-speaking child.' Legion replied.

'What are the chances of it not working?' Jonny asked tentatively.

'Oh, very small.'

'Like the Planck or smaller like Legion's brain?'

'Legion's brain,' Rapture replied, laughing.

'Ok, then let's do this,' Jonny said as he grabbed Legend's paw in his right hand and Legion's paw in his left.

Suddenly, Rapture began to shake so violently that Jonny thought all his teeth might fall out, and then, it stopped as soon as it started.

'We're there,' were Rapture's only words.

Jonny, Legend, and Legion stood in gobsmacked silence, not only because of the immense distance they had travelled but also because of the silly amount of time it had taken — literally one Earth second.

'My God,' exclaimed Legend. Jonny and Legion stood spellbound, almost unable to breathe.

'That... that's Dark Shadow?' Jonny finally asked.

'Well, a small part of it, yes, that is Dark Shadow,' Rapture whispered, adding, 'beautiful, isn't it?'

'I was thinking large rather than beautiful, but yes, it is also beautiful and, erm, large,' Jonny replied.

'No, that's way bigger than large,' Legion said as all three stood motionless, trying to take in what they could see.

'How far away are we?' Jonny asked, looking up, then down and from side to side.

'Oh, just about one million miles away.'

'What!!!'

'One million miles; if we arrived any closer, Dark Shadow would have detected us.'

'What, from one million miles?'

'Further, if we had come the normal way.'

'What, by bus?' Legend said, giggling.

'You know, Legend, if you took a bus from the bottom of your road to here, it would take longer to get here than it took to create your universe.'

'Imagine the fuel bill,' Jonny added, still unable to take his eyes off the stunning, jaw-dropping sight before him.

'Who or what lives here?' Legion asked tentatively.

'What would you think if I told you that every known and unknown species that has ever existed lived here?' Rapture replied.

'You mean everything that has EVER lived, including dinosaurs?' Legion asked inquisitively.

'Yes, including dinosaurs.'

'Everything, you mean everything that ever lived?' Jonny asked, still unable to imagine what could be down there. 'There's a short-sighted dinosaur called Doyouthinkhesawus,' Legion said, giggling.

'And one called Diploppypants,' Legend added.

'Actually, it's Diplodocus,' Jonny said matter-of-factly, but Legend and Legion weren't listening, too busy rolling around the floor, giggling.

'What about Pantywearingdraco?' Legend added.

'Or a Troodon – can you imagine being trod on by a Troodon?' Legion replied.

'Well, if that's bad, what about the Supersaurus?' Legend said, almost unable to breathe for giggling.

'Yes, I have a Supersaurus,' Legion replied in absolute hysterics.

'So, what do we do now, apart from ignoring these two imbeciles?' Jonny asked.

'Well, Jonny, I have managed to find out where we must go, but we must be quick.'

'Is that why you were sent to help us because you're so quick?'

'Yes, because I can travel so fast, we wouldn't be detected arriving or leaving, but, as I said, we have to move quickly, and Jonny, you have to practice your invisible-to-visible skills and learn to do it in total silence.'

'Did you hear that, numb-nuts? In total silence,' Jonny shouted, but Legend and Legion were too far gone, still rolling around in childish hysterics.

Jonny immediately disappeared, but Legend's and Legion's ears are far superior to humans.

'We both heard you try again,' Legend said, wiping the laughter tears from his face. Jonny tried repeatedly, but he was heard each time he became invisible.

'This isn't so easy,' Jonny said from apparently nowhere.

'Can still hear you,' Legion said, smiling.

'Yes, I know you can hear me, you fur ball.'

'Try doing it while holding your breath and closing your eyes,' Rapture suggested.

'Yes, and not talking,' Legion quipped. Jonny tried and tried, and each time he tried, he could be heard.

'Ok, now try the embryo position,' Rapture said gently.

'Did you hear me?' Jonny asked as he stood behind Legion, making him jump out of his skin.

'NO,' they all replied, and then Legend added, 'Keep doing it, but stop the scary stuff, ok?'

Jonny kept practising it until he had perfected it, but he had to do this while holding the Elixir of Life. Jonny looked around for something to carry; there was nothing apart from Legend's and Legion's collars made from stars. Jonny removed both of their collars and tried again.

'Heard you,' Legend whispered. Jonny tried again, holding the collars first in his right hand, then left. He then tied them around his foot, then neck, and finally, after he was about to give up, he took off his t-shirt and wrapped them both up tightly. Jonny tried again, but this time appeared behind Legend and stood silently and invisibly, and Legend hadn't noticed.

'That seems to work,' Jonny said to himself.

'Ok, well, then we must go. Hold on,' Rapture whispered. Then, with an incredible burst of astonishing power, Rapture moved across the black night sky and hovered, invisibly and deathly silent, high above Dark Shadow.

'Jonny, this is the plan: you have to go alone. I had hoped you could get help from Legend and Legion, but as you know, they're not the quietest of animals. What you need to do is take off your shoes and socks. Then tie your t-shirt tightly around your waist— and I mean tightly, so nothing can flap as you fly down to Dark Shadow. Once we are above the Hypericosahedron, you have to leave invisibly. Now, we are looking for a lake, but not a normal one. This lake is made from mercury, and it's quite deep.'

'How deep exactly?' Jonny asked, searching for a lake made of mercury.

'One thousand miles.'

'Oh, is that all? For a moment, I thought you would say it was one mile deep, but one thousand miles. How am I supposed to travel one thousand miles through mercury in the dark?'

'Hold your breath,' Legend added unhelpfully.

* * * * * * *

Meanwhile, back at Class 1a, one very excited Gracie had just been informed that, due to her insane football abilities, she would be allowed to play in one of the most important football games of her life.

'Gracie, you can get changed in my office because you cannot get changed in the changing room. The bus leaves in one hour. Be ready and waiting by the school gates,' Miss Kitkat boomed across the hushed classroom, then added, 'Perhaps tie your hair up; it will make you look more boyish.'

'Yes, Miss,' Gracie replied, still unable to remove the enormous grin that seemed permanently stuck to her young face. The stinky old-school bus waited as the team quietly got on board. Many were surprised to see Gracie sitting at the back of the bus, grinning from ear to ear.

'Oi, that's where we sit,' Melon face shouted.

'No, that's where you used to sit, Melon face. Now I'm sitting here instead of Jonny Plumb,' Gracie replied, still smiling.

'You cheeky little...'

'Leave her alone,' Biffo Brown shouted as he pushed his way to the back of the bus and sat down next to the still-grinning Gracie, adding, 'Ignore them; you're part of the team now.'

'OUCH, who did that?' Melon's face shouted as some invisible force slapped him hard on his cheeks.

'OUCH, stop doing that,' he shouted, looking around him, much to everyone's amusement.

The old, stinky school bus pulled outside the gates of the most dreadful-looking school. Massive gothic high spires pointed skywards. It was the most dismal school you could ever wish to attend. The school captain and head boy, also known as Mad Mucky Micky, were waiting at the gates. He looked like he had just emerged from a lunatic asylum. His long hair is uncombed, and his facial hair makes him look much older than sixteen, sixty-six more like. Soon, he was joined by a gaggle of equally ugly, wall-eyed, insane boys who all began to howl like wolves do on a full moon.

'Ignore them,' Biffo Brown shouted as he jumped off the coach. Without saying please, Biffo Brown pushed the massive school gates open, but unbeknown to him, he had caught Mucky Mental Mickey's foot under the enormous metal gate. He howled in pain, but no one took any notice as they all thought he was still leading the chorus of howling. Nanny Noo was the last off the coach, and as she floated past him, she slapped him so hard he passed out.

'One down, ten to go,' she whispered to the ape beside her.

'Who said that?' he shouted, looking to his left and right.

'I did,' Nanny Noo replied and punched him so hard in the stomach that he fell to the ground, almost unable to breathe.

'Just nine to go,' Nanny Noo said, giggling as she pulled the most horrendous face and screamed like a deranged banshee right into the face of their six-foot-six-inch goalkeeper.

'Agh, what in God's name was that?' he screamed and ran off across the playing fields and hid in the bushes, shaking with fear.

Both teams arrived on the dodgy-looking pitch to a cacophony of noise, but one team was missing a few players. The captain had been carted off to hospital with a badly cut foot. The mammoth of a goalkeeper was trembling so much that he could hardly walk. Floppy Leg still had a nasty case of floppy leg and arrived in a wheelchair, and to spice things up, Nanny Noo had poked their defender Peter Plank in the eye, and he now wore an eye patch. Things were looking up for West House, and things were going to get even better thanks to two mischievous spirits known as Nanny Noo and her husband, Stan.

* * * * * * *

'It appears to know we are here,' Rapture said while Jonny, Legend and Legion stood staring in amazement at the size of everything.

'How do you mean?' Jonny asked.

'It has sent a message.'

'Who has sent a message?'

'Dark Shadow has.'

'How can a land mass send messages?'

'I am unsure, but I am receiving a message.'

'What's it say?'

'Just a series of numbers.'

'Numbers?'

'Yes, numbers.'

'How many numbers, Rapture?'

'Nineteen.'

'What are these numbers?'

'1-1-2-3-5-8-13-21-34-55-89-144-233-377-610-987-1597-2584-4181.'

'Fibonacci scale,' Jonny said, adding, 'if you drew little squares with these numbers as the widths, you would get a spiral. Here, let me show you.'

'Like this, do you mean?' Rapture said as she showed everyone the shape.

'Yes, that's it.'

'Don't know why it's called the Fibonacci Scale as he didn't invent it, as it was done hundreds of years before, in India, way before he was even born,' Jonny said then with a quick calculation in his head said, 'those numbers all add up to 10945. I wonder what that means.'

'Perhaps it's telling us how to get to the Hypericosahedron,' Legend said.

'I was just about to say that,' Legion added, grinning.

'You don't think it's a trap, do you, Rapture?' Jonny asked while deciphering the many numbers in his head.

'I think it's showing us how to get into the Hypericosahedron...'

'Der, I just said that,' Legend butted in.

'...Using the spaceship,' Rapture replied patiently.

'Yes, and those numbers are a code to get in, but get into what?' Jonny said, scratching his head.

'I wasn't expecting this,' Rapture said, sounding almost surprised at the ingenuity of this vast land mass.

'I think I have an answer to the numbers,' Jonny said, almost pleased with himself, adding, 'I remember my dad telling how security checks were done in the army; the guard would shout out a number to anyone coming near, and if the person gave the wrong number, they were, err, shot.'

'Please explain,' Rapture asked.

'Well, the known number was always nine, so if the guard shouted four, then the correct response would be five, and if he shouted seven, the answer would be two and so on.'

'I see, so that the new numbers would be 8-8-7-6-4-1-5-7-2-8-1-0-1-1-2-3-5-9-4,' Rapture replied instantly.

'You learn quickly, Rapture. Well, let's send back this sequence of numbers and see what happens, but be careful, I still think it could be a trap.'

'What? I don't understand,' Legend said as he looked at Legion.

'It's the difference between the numbers they sent and the number nine.'

'Oh, good, so glad we cleared that up,' Legion laughed.

'Ok, what's the difference between the number one and nine?'

'Eight,' Legend and Legion replied in unison, both very happy they got the question right.

'So that was easy, wasn't it?'

'Easy-ish,' Legion replied.

'Dark Shadow has replied.'

'What did it say, Rapture?' Jonny asked.

'Intrare in Raptu.'

'What does "enter a rabbit" mean?' Legend said, giggling.

'Only enter in Rapture.'

'Rapture, ask them why.'

'Or.'

'Or, what, Rapture?'

'Jonny mortietur.'

'Or, what, Jonny?' Legend asked.

'Jonny will die,' Rapture replied.

'Oh,' said Legend.

'So, the only way we can get to the Hypericosahedron is from inside Rapture?'

'Yes, it would appear so, plus we have to use the Fibonacci scale to plot our flight path.'

'What about the numbers?'

'I guess there must be something down there that needs these numbers, like a lock.'

'I don't get this, and I don't trust this. Rapture, please ask Dark Shadow again what the numbers are for.'

'Liberare elixer vitae,' Rapture replied.

'To free the elixir of life,' Jonny whispered, adding, ' This seems too easy. I am sure it's a trap.'

'For something so valuable, they seem very relaxed about giving it up,' Legend said.

'Yes, perhaps we should ask them, Rapture.'

'Ok, I have sent a message asking why and Dark Shadow replied, "to help mankind reach enlightenment."'

'Makes sense, I guess. What use is it if it's not doing some good?' Jonny replied.

'They just replied, "Exactly,"' Rapture said in astonishment.

'How on earth did they know what I was saying?'

'I am Dark Shadow,' a booming voice echoed, engulfing Rapture.

'Who said that?' Legend asked.

'I am Dark Shadow.'

'Who are you?' Legion added.

'I am Dark Shadow.'

'But what are...'

'...Legend, Legion, forget the twenty questions. I have been in a similar position with Darkness. Don't ask any more questions because you will get the same reply whatever you say,' Jonny interrupted Legend mid-sentence.

'I am Dark Shadow...'

'...See, I told you,' Jonny said, laughing.

'I am Dark Shadow, and you must collect the Elixir of life now or lose it forever.'

'Good God, look,' Legend yelled as he pointed towards the vast lake made of Mercury.

'My God, the lake of Mercury has changed into a giant whirlpool,' Jonny said in mild shock.

'I am Dark Shadow; you must follow the coordinates of the Fibonacci scale to arrive at the Hypericosahedron. It will open for a millisecond and then close. Close forever.'

Rapture quickly plotted a course while Jonny put his socks, shoes and trousers back on.

'I am Dark Shadow. When you reach the Hypericosahedron, you must whisper the numbers you have deciphered. If you fail or make one mistake, the Hypericosahedron will imprison you for the rest of time. You have ten seconds. 10- 9...'

'Jonny, you know the numbers?' Legend asked in mild hysteria.

'Err,'

'No, not err, Jonny, dumb.'

'8-8-7-6-4-1-5-7-2-8-1-0-1-1-2-3-5-9-4,' Jonny replied.

'8-7-6' the countdown continued.

Rapture flew a million miles to the surface of Dark Shadow in a thousandth of a second and then into the gigantic whirlpool made from Mercury.

'Anyone else here feels ever so slightly scared?' Legend asked.

'W-M-P,' Legion replied.

'What does that mean?' Legend asked.

'Wet My Pants,' Legion replied, shaking.

'5-4-3.'

In a millisecond, Rapture arrived and floated silently. The noise of the spinning whirlpool was almost deafening, even from inside Rapture's safety. Suddenly, in front of them was this giant— and I mean huge—machine known as the Hypericosahedron, and an eerie silence fell.

'3-2.'

'8-8-7-6-4-1-5-7-2-8-1-0-1-1-2-3-5-9-4,' Jonny whispered.

'I am Dark Shadow; what is the total of these numbers?' '82,' Jonny blurted out.

'I am Dark Shadow, you are incorrect.'

Without a moment's hesitation, Jonny whispered, '1'.

'I am Dark Shadow... You are correct.'

* * * * * * *

To escape the gravitational forces of Dark Shadow, Rapture had to accelerate at ten times the speed of light. The considerable whirlpool made from Mercury silently stopped, and the lake resumed its usual calm within seconds.

'How did you know the answer was "1" Jonny?' Rapture asked.

'Pure guess,' Jonny replied, 'pure guess.'

'I don't understand how you could guess the correct number,' Legend asked, sidling up to Jonny.

'I added the last two numbers as I had already added the rest, such as I added all these numbers   8-8-7-6-4-1-5-7-2-8-1-0-1-1-2-3-5-9-4, which made 82. I just added them together, 8+2 = 10 = 1. Just a lucky guess, I guess.'

'You know Jonny, I don't know where you learnt to be so laidback and brave, but that was an incredible risk. We were one second away from death,' Rapture said, almost in awe.

'Perhaps I haven't learnt to fear everything, as adults seem to do,' Jonny replied and passed out.

'I am Dark Shadow. Jonny Plumb, you are my friend,' words echoed around Rapture as she accelerated to ten thousand times the speed of light and back towards home.

* * * * * * *

Three players down, and the Mucky Mental Marauders already looked like a beaten team. Stan stood on the away team's goal line with strict instructions; 'do not let the ball into the net' resounding in his ears. The whistle blew, and the crowd roared, but not for long, as Nanny Noo set about seeking vengeance for Jonny. As soon as one of the home team players got the ball, she would repeatedly slap them until a member of West House ran up and nicked the ball. The ball was neatly passed around the team like seasoned professionals.

Quick one-pass football left the home team bemused and chasing shadows. The ball was passed to Gracie, who no one had realised was a girl, who then did what she excelled at, running and dribbling with astonishing speed. She even had time to nutmeg two players, and when they tried to kick her back, she got slapped several times by Nanny Noo, who loved every second. Gracie jinked this way, then that, and unleashed a shot so hard no goalkeeper in the world could have saved it. One - Nil to West House, and the silence was deafening.

Heads began to fall, and to brighten things up, Nanny Noo flew from player to player, slapping them repeatedly in the face. Then she made one player slap the player next to him. Of course, being a bit thick, he began fighting with his teammates, and while they did, Gracie scored a second goal. Two-Nil to West House.

Now, angry, the home team began to play a decent bit of football, but sadly, a steady chorus of boos came from their supporters. One player managed to get a shot on goal, and it was heading right into the right-hand of the goal; well, that was until the ball suddenly and unexpectedly stopped on the line. The goalkeeper just casually picked the ball up and kicked it upfield to Fat Wallet, who, without really knowing what he was doing, just kicked it as hard as it could, only to land at the feet of Nanny Noo, who smashed the ball into the back of the net. Unbelievable score, Three-Nil to West House. The referee blew for the end of the first half, and the home team rushed up to complain about the game, but what could the referee do, as he could see nothing was wrong?

'Right in the second half, just try and keep the ball, nothing flash as I really cannot see them scoring,' Biffo Brown said to all the players.

While he chatted away, Nanny Noo walked up behind the home team's goalkeeper and, taking the goalkeeper's hand, she slapped the referee very hard around the back of his head.

'I never touched him,' the goalkeeper shouted, adding, 'I never touched you, ref, honest.' The linesman ran over and whispered in the referee's ear, 'The goalkeeper hit you with his right hand; it's a red card offence.'

The referee took the red card from his pocket and, to the goalkeeper's and team's utter dismay, sent the innocent goalkeeper off. Four players down, and Nanny Noo was playing havoc and enjoying every second while Stan stood in the goal, not allowing anything past him.

The whistle blew for the second half, and immediately, Biffo Brown won the ball fairly. He passed it to Billy Cartwright, who had been relatively subdued until now. He played a beautiful one-two with Biffo Brown and then passed a defence-splitting ball to Gracie, who had run almost the entire length of the pitch to smash in a screamer of a goal: Four-Nil and a hat-trick for the pitch's youngest, smallest, and girliest player.

The home team looked shattered, but in all fairness to them, they did try, but every goal-bound shot was mysteriously stopped by Stan, who was in his element. Again and again, they kicked the ball towards an empty net as the goalkeeper produced a mirror from his kitbag and preened himself. Again and again, Stan saved everything. Morale was low, but it was just about to get much worse. The goalkeeper picked the ball up and kicked it as hard as he could; with some wind assistance or Nanny Noo assistance, the ball landed at Biffo Brown's right foot, and he unleashed a shot that was so powerful that ten brick walls couldn't have stopped it. Five-Nil, yes, Five-Nil. The referee blew for full-time, and West House went crazy.

Quickly, they all jumped back into the rickety, stinky old school bus and drove home, but before they left the gates, Gracie let her long blond hair down and tossed it to and from in front of the angry school supporters. Then, she blew kisses at them as the bus trundled home, and they all sang happily.

'News had somehow reached West House that their young, inexperienced football team had thrashed the Mucky Mental Marauders five-nil. The entire school came out of their classrooms to celebrate, and one little girl who stole the show was lifted shoulder high and carried up the slope to the school and awaiting staff to rapturous applause.'

CHAPTER TWO:
JONNY AND THE MACHINE

'Is that it?' Legend asked Jonny as he held the Elixir of Life in his tiny hands.

'Funny colour,' Legion added.

'So would you be if you were stuck in the Hippopsychowardatteatime for millions of years,' Legend said, giggling.

'You meant the Hypericosahedron?' Jonny replied.

'Yes, that's what I said, the Hypobladderfullofweetime,' Legend replied, laughing.

'It does look tiny though, doesn't it,' Legion said as he walked around Jonny, not taking his beady eyes off the Elixir, then adding, 'This small thing can cure every illness in the multiverse?'

'Only when it's put inside the machine Jonny has to build,' Rapture said gently.

'Crumbs, I had forgotten all about that.'

'We are about to bend space and time,' Rapture said, adding, 'Don't forget what happened last time.'

Jonny quickly placed the Elixir of Life into a beam of light, then grabbed Legend's paw in one hand and Legion's paw in the other. Rapture began to shake violently, and, in a millisecond, Rapture was silently floating in Jonny's back garden.

'Haven't you gone yet?' Sir Ranulf asked in bewilderment as Jonny, Legend, and Legion emerged through the walls of Rapture.

'Hi Dad, Hi Mum, Hi Nanny Carole, Hi Charlie, Hi Nanny Noo, Hi Stan,' Jonny said cheerily as he walked towards his Mum.

'What's that you're holding, Jonny?' Nanny Carole asked as she looked intently at the smallish sphere in Jonny's hands. 'This, Nanny Carole, is the Elixir of Life,' Jonny said proudly.

'Looks like a second-hand, skin-coloured netball to me,' Nanny Carole replied before vanishing back into the house.

'I expected something more than "it looks like a second-hand skin-coloured netball to me,"' Jonny said, almost disappointedly.

'Dad, can I ring, or can you ring Professor Ziad?'

'Yes, of course you can. Hold on, where's that spaceship gone?'

Jonny turned around to see that Rapture had vanished into thin air. Jonny stood quietly, still holding onto the Elixir of Life, then whispered, 'I think I'm going to have a bath and then go to sleep.'

* * * * * * *

Jonny ran a nice, soothing, hot bath. He effortlessly slid in while the most valuable item in all the multiverses sat precariously at the end of the tub, looking like the second-hand, skin-coloured netball that Nanny Carole had so described before.

Suddenly, there was a whoosh as all the sea life erupted out of the water to greet Jonny.

'Jonny, where have you been? Have you missed us?' Sloppy Botty asked, letting rip a real nose-curler of a parp.

'Well, I have missed you all, but I haven't missed your rotten bottom, Sloppy Botty. I thought you were cured.'

'Actually, Jonny, I enjoy it.'

'Yeah, but we don't,' all the sea life replied in unison.

'Whoa, what is that?' Sloppy Botty asked, staring at the Elixir of Life, then added, 'I know, don't tell me; you have taken up playing netball, haven't you?'

'That, Sloppy Botty, is the most valuable thing...'

'...Netball!' Sloppy Botty interrupted, swimming up to the most valuable artefact in the world and prodding it with his long nose.

'...No, my God, what is wrong with everybody today? I have just travelled a journey that no one or thing has or ever will travel to the magical, mysterious, magnificent Dark Shadow. Then I conquered my fear of death by not being caught or being swallowed by the truly amazing Hypericosahedron.'

'It's a netball, Jonny,' all the Sea Life replied.

'Sorry, Jonny, where did you say you have just been to?' Wall-Eyed Wally asked as he set about washing Jonny's hair.

'I have been to Dark Shadow,' Jonny replied.

'Oh, that's just a made-up story, it doesn't exist,' Porka the Orca added.

'It is Heaven, isn't it, Jonny?' Squelch said softly.

'Yes, it is known as Heaven, and every kind of animal that ever lived in the entire multiverses lives there,' Jonny replied.

'So, let me get this straight,' Sloppy Botty said as he looked Jonny directly in the eye, then added, 'you travelled further than any person has ever, ever, ever done before to a place that doesn't exist, well only in your silly mind, to collect a netball?'

'It's not a netball; it's the Elixir of Life.'

'Watch this,' Sloppy Botty said as he balanced the most valuable treasure in the entire multiverse on his long nose. He tossed it high and balanced it again on his nose. Suddenly, Sloppy Botty stopped as the Elixir of Life began to change colour. He gently placed it back on the edge of the bath and swam back a few feet to where all the other Sea Life had quietly congregated.

'Th-th-the netball's changing colour,' Porka the Orca stammered.

'And shape,' Faraway added.

A ray of the most incredible colour shot out of the fast-changing sphere and seemed to caress Sloppy Botty, sending him into an absolute rapture. He smiled a contented smile. From that moment and for the rest of Sloppy Botty's life, he would thankfully no longer parp. One by one, each sea life was caressed by this gentle, loving, beautiful light, and one by one, you could see pure ecstasy written across their smiling faces. Then the light engulfed Jonny, gently rocking him from side to side as a mother does to a newborn baby. Jonny closed his eyes and felt genuine love for the first time. Unstoppable tears ran down his and all the Sea Life's faces. No words were said as they all relaxed in the most beautifully serene feelings known to man.

'This is how you feel when you depart from this world and into the next,' Jonny said ever so slowly and then added, 'and when the egg is fertilised, this is how the beginning of life in the womb feels for all creatures. This is perfection.' Jonny took the multicoloured sphere and swam down to where the Golden Globe was still resting on its pedestal. Then, something that Jonny had never witnessed before, the Golden Globes opened just like a flowering rose, and the Elixir of Life gently floated inside. The Golden Globe gently and effortlessly closed its petals around the sphere, and it was gone.

'I'll tell you all about Dark Shadow another time, but now I must sleep as I am completely shattered,' Jonny said as he jumped out of the hot bath and waved to all the sea life, who seemed very laid back and as yet Sloppy Botty hadn't let rip.

* * * * * * *

'Jonny, now you must create the machine which shall be called, well, Jonny, seeing you risked your life on more than one occasion, in fact several, I think it only fair that you get to name it,' Cosmos whispered as Jonny lay on his bed.

'Wow.'

'You're going to call this life-saving machine, "Wow", are you Jonny?' Legion said, giggling.

'Perhaps I should name it after you.'

'Oh yes, please. I can see it now, Legion the...'

'...Numbnuts,' Jonny butted in, destroying Legion's dream.

'What about Legend?' Legend said, raising his head proudly to the sky, in that posing look only large Rottweilers can do and get away with.

'I know, what about Legion and Legend?' Legion said while mimicking Legend.

'Ahem, don't you mean Legend and Legion?' Legend replied.

'No, no, I think you will find it should be Legion and then Legend,' Legion retorted.

'Alphabetically, I come first.'

'Egoistically, you do.'

'Ugliness, you do.'

'Ladies, if you wouldn't mind. I don't think calling a life-giving machine that can also cure all known and unknown illnesses in the entire multiverse after two quarrelling dogs would work, do you?'

'Yes,' Legend and Legion replied.

'Well, it's good to see you finally agree on something.'

'So, as you're not going to call this thing by my name or Legend's, what will you call it?'

'I'm not too sure.'

'Well, that's a ridiculous name; even my name's better than that,' Legion said, laughing.

'Shamayin is a nice word,' Jonny replied, adding, 'It means heaven.'

'What about "Heaven on Earth"?' Legend suggested.

'HOE,' Legion said, giggling.

'You can't call it a Hoe, you dim dog,' Jonny replied, adding, 'That's something a gardener would use. I must sleep; perhaps we can think of a good name in our sleep.'

'Dog snot,' Legend said, laughing.

'Dog bogies,' Legion added.

'Morons,' Jonny said as he wrapped himself in the warm blanket and fell fast asleep.

* * * * * * *

'So, Jonny, can you explain why you told all of us you were going to go to a distant land called, er...'

'Dark Shadow, Dad,' Jonny interrupted.

'... Yes, Dark Shadow, but you went nowhere except into a light beam and returned with an old netball.'

'Did you ring Professor Ziad, Dad?' Jonny asked, choosing to ignore the other questions.

'Yes, I did, about an hour ago, coming over for a spot of tea. Are you going to show him your netball, Jonny?'

'Stop teasing the boy, Ranulf. Anyway, it's lovely netball, isn't it, Jonny? So glad you have taken up a girl's sport,' Lady Kathleen said as she wafted in and out of the kitchen while blowing on her newly manicured blood-red nails.

'I must have returned to the year sarcastic,' Jonny mumbled.

'What was that, old boy?'

'Oh, nothing, Dad, it doesn't matter, does it?'

'What doesn't matter, old stick? Come on, cheer up, we can all play netball later if you like. I must fly off to see if I can still fly the old kite for the flypast over Bucks Palace.'

'And in English, please,' Jonny said, annoyed that no one seemed to care or believe where he had been.

'I have, well, I and other members of my old squadron, well, the ones who are still alive, have been asked to fly our Spitfires and Hurricanes and one or two Lancaster Bombers over Buckingham Palace and down The Mall. Might be room for one more if you play your cards right.'

'No, it's alright; I must build an, err, erm...'

'Dog snot,' Legend butted in, laughing.

'You have to build dog snot? How on earth can you do that? Anyway, I must dash. Good luck with the netball, Jonny. Toodlepip, old sausage,' Sir Ranulf shouted as he put on his old leather flying jacket and goggles and then marched out of the front door to be joined by Sir Harry Taylor.

'Thought of a good name for the machine yet, Jonny?' Legion asked.

'Jonny, you forgot to tell me about Dark Shadow and why you didn't go,' Sir Ranulf said as he came back into the kitchen to pick up his flying gloves from the kitchen sideboard.

'Dad, I did go; I flew trillions of miles in that beam of light, as you call her. I diced with death and outsmarted the Hypericosahedron. I flew at ten thousand times the speed of light, and I returned with the elixir of life or netball, as you describe it, exactly one minute after I left, and now I have to build a machine. All I wanted, Dad, was someone to believe me,' Jonny stood up, walked out of the door and ran to school with tears rolling down his face, followed as ever by his two most loyal companions and best friends, Legend and Legion.

'Jonny, wait a moment,' Legend said, placing his massive paw on Jonny's tiny shoulders, 'They don't understand, Jonny. These are just simple folks who have little understanding of what you're about and cannot begin to understand your complexities and the life you have been chosen to lead. Give them time and be patient. Now off you go to school, see you tonight.'

Jonny smiled and hugged Legend and Legion, whispering, 'I don't know where I would be without you two. I love you more than life.'

'And we love you more than life as well,' Legend and Legion replied as one, as they turned to go home as soon as the school gates came into view.

'Hello Jonny, did you hear? We won, and I scored a hat trick,' Gracie said proudly as she carefully slid a note inside Jonny's school jacket.

'You must be pleased,' Jonny replied, not wanting to talk nor wanting to be rude; he just smiled and walked past and headed towards the school.

'Bye Jonny, I love you, Jonny,' Gracie shouted so everyone could hear.

'Bye Jonny, we love you,' Fat Wallet and his thick friends added playfully.

'I saw him before you,' Plug and Pillock shouted, teasing. However, Jonny wasn't in the mood for anything, not even school. Miss Kitkat ordered everyone to 'be upstanding' as the Music Teacher, Miss Harridan, plonked on what sounded like 'Michael Rowed the Boat Ashore' on the old school piano. The school sang with gusto and pride, which took Jonny by surprise.

'Why's everyone so happy?' Jonny whispered to the person sitting beside him without looking to see who it was.

'They won the football match,' a familiar voice replied.

'Isobel,' Jonny said, startled.

'Jonny,' Isobel replied.

'Isobel, I thought you were in Scotland with your Auntie McHaggis McPlop.'

'I was, but I escaped, slid down a rope made out of knotted sheets, and then ran to the station in my nightie and hid on the parcel shelf.'

'What?'

'Only joking, Jonny. I'm down for a week and must return next weekend.' Isobel looked at Jonny briefly, then said, 'Did you miss me?'

'Err, yes, yes, of course, I missed you,' Jonny replied hesitantly.

'You don't seem very happy to see me.'

'I am, honestly, but like I said, I just wasn't expecting you.'

'I brought you a present from Scotland. I will put it in your pocket, and you can see it later.' Isobel placed the small box in Jonny's pocket, and as she pulled her hand out, the note Gracie had written fell out. Isobel quickly picked it up and was about to put it back in Jonny's pocket when she saw something that made her change her mind. The words read...

'To the one I love,' written in red with kisses all over the envelope. Isobel quickly turned the pink, sweet-smelling envelope over and saw S.W.A.L.K written in large lettering. Isobel quickly took the envelope and placed it inside her hymnbook.

'Walk me home after school?' Isobel asked sweetly, then pecked Jonny on the cheek and left with her giggling school friends to the day's first lesson, home economics, and Jonny went off to his Metalwork class.

Jonny couldn't wait to go home and, in his rush, almost forgot to wait for Isobel.

'Who is Gracie?' Isobel asked.

'I dunno,' Jonny replied as they slowly strolled down the leafy lanes towards Isobel's home.

'Gracie,' Isobel added.

'No idea,' Jonny replied, his hands pushed deep in his trouser pockets while nonchalantly kicking the autumn leaves.

'Oh, hold on, she played instead of me in the football match. Why do you ask?'

'Why didn't you play?'

'I got a three-match ban for ungentlemanly behaviour on the field of play.'

'Did you fart?'

'No, I did not fart,' Jonny replied laughing, 'I just gave a thug, floppy leg, that's all, teach him a lesson.'

'So, what's wrong with that?'

'I forgot to unfloppy his floppy legs, and because I forgot to unfloppy his floppy legs, a series of unforeseen accidents happened.'

'Such as?'

'A house burnt down.'

'What! How?'

'Well, ok, if you must know. He, who had a floppy leg, had to be carried home on a stretcher. When his wife saw him, she fainted and squashed the cat; the cat ran away and hit a paraffin lamp.

The paraffin lamp fell over onto the curtains, and the curtains caught fire and set the house alight. The fire brigade was called and put out the fire, but everything they owned was ruined; plus, the cat won't come home because it got burnt by the paraffin lamp that it knocked over after it was squashed by its owner fainting due to seeing her husband being wheeled in on a stretcher and all because I gave the guy, who was playing football, a floppy leg. Plus, the cat, a rare Persian cat, had never returned, and the cat wasn't insured. Therefore, I get a three-match ban.'

'Ok, so where does this Gracie fit in?'

'What's with all the questions about Gracie, Isobel?'

'Oh, nothing, just wondered.'

'Just wondering a lot. Do you know her then?'

'You know she's not well, don't you? And no, I don't know her?'

'How would I know if she was unwell? She was fit enough to play for the school football team, right?'

'I mean, she errs, has an err...' Isobel stuttered, 'An err? Sounds jolly painful.'

'Life-threatening.'

'She has a life-threatening err?'

'No, Jonny, she has a life-threatening illness, and she hasn't got long to live.' Jonny stopped and looked Isobel straight in the eye and said, 'You said that you didn't know her, yet you seem to know all about her, how?'

'Oh Jonny, I'm sorry.'

'What for, my little bluebell?'

'For taking this.'

'Taking what?'

'You know in assembly, I told you I had put a little present in your pocket?'

'Oh, I forgot,' Jonny then placed his hand in his pocket and pulled out a small pink box.

'No, forget that.'

'What?'

'Jonny, the letter is in your pocket, and I took it out.'

'What letter in my pocket?'

'This one.' Jonny looked puzzled as Isobel waved the tiny pink, sweet-smelling, perfumed envelope in front of his face.

'Is that from you?'

'No, Jonny, it's from Gracie's mother.'

'Hold on, if that's from Gracie's mother, why has it got S.W.A.L.K written on it and covered in little crosses?'

'Kisses, Jonny, they're kisses,'

'Kisses? Why would her...'

'...Her Mother wrote you a letter, and I guess Gracie wrote on the envelope.' Isobel butted in.

'It's open,' Jonny said as he gently took the envelope from Isobel's grasp.

'I know. I opened it; oh God, I'm sorry, Jonny. I was just jealous, that's all. I thought you had found a new girlfriend and didn't love me anymore.' Jonny took the note out of the opened envelope and read it to himself.

'Dearest Jonny, let me introduce myself. My name is Patricia, and I am Gracie's mother. Gracie hasn't stopped talking about you ever since she met you; she tells me that you helped her fulfil a lifetime's dream to play a full game of football. You see, Jonny, Gracie has a rare heart condition for which there is no known cure. She says that without your help and the help of your father, she wouldn't have had the courage even to try. Her father and I had always hoped that she would fulfil her dreams, and thanks to you, she has. We are unsure exactly how much time our beloved Gracie has left. We just wanted to write to say thank you. With much love, from Patricia & Frank.'

Jonny wiped the tears that freely ran down his face and looked directly at Isobel as he placed the perfectly written note back into the pink envelope, but his hands shook so much that he could not.

'Here, let me do that,' Isobel said gently.

'I must help her,' Jonny mumbled.

'Yes, Jonny, you must.'

* * * * * * *

'Professor, I need your help, but you must be serious, listen, understand and not laugh. Do you think you can do that?' Jonny asked.

'Yes, of course I can, but why the long face? Have you turned into a horse?' Professor Ziad said, laughing.

'You failed at being serious, Professor.'

'Only joking with you, young Jonny. Now, I will be serious. See, Jonny, this is my serious face. So, what exactly is it that you need help with?'

'Being serious might help.'

'I promise, scout's honour.'

'Ok, well, I have to build a machine.'

'Ooh, how exciting! What's it going to be called?'

'I'm not sure.'

'Ok, unusual name, but you know best, old chicken.'

'No, I am unsure what to call it.'

'Well, I suggest you don't name it after my wife, eh, Jonny. Anyway, joking aside, what does this machine do?'

'It will cure all known illnesses and make sad people happy.'

'Oh, like the one hundred phials you cleverly have hidden under your bed?'

'Yes, but better, as it cures ALL KNOWN ILLNESSES.'

'With you so far, old turkey. I have to place certain objects in a certain way to make it work.'

'Like the parts of a clock. By themselves, they do nothing, but collectively, they can tell the time.'

'Spot on, Professor, spot on, and when done, build a safe home for it.'

'A very safe home by the sounds of it. I mean, what would this thing be worth?'

'Priceless.'

'Worth dying for?'

'Rather.'

'Oh dear.'

'Why, oh dear?'

'The knobby reptile.'

'You mean the Gnud Repeek, Professor.'

'Ah yes, him as well. So, we must build something that doesn't look or have a name that sounds like the greatest healing machine on earth.'

'Yep.'

'Mmmmm, not easy.'

'But can be done, right Professor?'

'Right, Jonny, so what and where are all the parts? I had better write them all down.'

Thirteen singing rune stones,

A single hair from Stump Grinding,

A tear from Isobel,

The rose petal from the Queen of Iceland,

The shard of pure light,

The Golden Globe,

One very sharp shark's tooth,

The one-ring,

Lord's Prayer, written in Aramaic,

The one hundred phials.

'You have all these safely hidden then?' the Professor asked as he quickly jotted down the parts.

'Yep.'

'So where is the fabled Elixir of Life? Don't tell me, under your bed and all the other parts?'

'No, it's erm, inside the Golden Globe and the Shard of Pure Light.'

'Hard to believe that the most valuable thing in the world...'

'Multiverse,' Jonny butted in.

'...is in an old cast-iron tub.'

'Yeah, amazing, eh?'

'Jonny, do you know what a franchise is?'

'Erm, is that where I allow others to sell my stuff, but I keep my name or product, and I take a percentage?'

'More or less, Jonny. Now, can you imagine creating this machine and then selling it across the world?'

'Professor, I am not interested in money; I never have and never will. I want to create a machine to help cure the sick and not give it to the highest bidder, but you have a point which has given me an idea.'

'Which is?'

'I'll tell you tomorrow, but first, I need to go and check Sloppy Botty's botty.'

'Wouldn't you prefer a nice glass of ginger beer and a slice of cake instead?'

'Not now, Professor, tomorrow perhaps,' Jonny said as he ran out of the kitchen and up the stairs to run a soothing hot bath and to think.

* * * * * * *

'What do you mean Sloppy Botty has stopped parping? I don't believe you,' Jonny said in disbelief.

'Well, ask him then if you don't believe us,' Wall-Eyed Wally said, climbing on Jonny's head to begin washing Jonny's hair.

'It's true, look, I have been trying to drop a nose curler, a bottom burp, a noisy mud monkey, a phrrap, a parp or even a teeny weenie squeak all day, but nothing happens, watch.' Sloppy Botty said as he did everything he possibly could to drop a smelly, release a stinker and fire the smelly machine gun, but nothing, absolutely nothing.

'Well, that's brilliant news,' Jonny said, smiling, adding, 'if that elixir can cure your bottom, Sloppy, I reckon it can cure anything, don't you?'

'But I don't want my bottom cured. I like phrraping.'

'Yes, Sloppy, I can understand that, but what about the rest of the sea life who have had to put up with your incurable bottom burping for years? You should be delighted.'

'Jonny, I can see,' Blue Sky One Eye said as she gently nudged Jonny.

'You mean out of both eyes?' Jonny said, smiling.

'Yes, I can see for the first time in ages.'

'Oh, Blue Sky, that's brilliant. Sloppy Botty, isn't that great news?'

'I want my bottom burps back,' Sloppy Botty said miserably.

'Think we will have to give you a new name now as Sloppy Botty isn't being Sloppy Botty anymore.'

'How about we call him Stroppy Botty?' Porca the Orca shouted, making everybody laugh. Well, everyone except Sloppy was in a proper mood.

'It's what I am, it's what I do, I fart, I enjoy farting, it makes me happy,' Stroppy Botty said, trying to explain himself, adding, 'What am I going to do now? I WANT TO FAAAAARRRRT, I want to fart.'

Stroppy Botty began crying uncontrollably; 'I just want to fart, just once more, just a little one, just a wee bubbly one.'

'Does everyone else feel good, as in better?' Jonny asked.

'YES,' was the single-word reply.

'So, by just being in the water with the netball, I mean the Elixir, it's not only healed Stroppy Botty's bottom, it's also cured Blue Sky's blind eye. I wonder, I wonder,' Jonny muttered as he leapt out of the bath and flicked water at Legend and Legion.

* * * * * * *

'Hi Gracie, sorry I wasn't very talkative the other day,' Jonny said as a steady stream of kids left school.

'Hi Jonny, did you read the note mother wrote?'

'Yes, I did, unsure what to say, except I might be able to help you.'

'Help me? How do you mean you could help me?'

'It's a secret, but if you trust me, would you like to come to my house someday? Perhaps I can help you improve your football skills.'

'Oh yes, yes please, oh God, I can't believe this, Jonny Plumb asking me to come to his house,' Gracie said, running off with her giggling school friends, turning every few seconds to wave at Jonny.

'How can you help her?' Isobel asked.

'Listen, Isobel, since the last time I saw you, I have gone on one of those crazy journeys I sometimes do.'

'Oh, did you get that final part of the jigsaw?'

'Yes.'

'And you have built the machine?'

'No, not yet, but when I hid the elixir in my bath, it seemed to have affected Sloppy Botty's bottom.'

'You're so funny, Jonny, hiding things in a bath as if. Who on earth is Sloppy Botty?'

'Ah, have I not told you about the sea life in my bath?'

'Err, no, Jonny, and if you did, I would think you had completely lost your marbles. It's ok, Jonny; you like to play games.'

'Yeah, like I have sea life in my bath.'

'So, what is this thing you got then?'

'It's called the Elixir of Life and can cure anyone of anything.'

'Like my mother?'

'Oh, I never thought about her, yes I suppose so.'

'And it can cure Gracie?'

'Yes, and Gracie.'

'Wow, let me see it,'

'I can't, it's hidden.'

'Oh yeah, I forgot, hidden in your bath.'

'You can keep a secret, can't you, Isobel?'

'You don't need to ask that, do you, Jonny?'

'When I placed the Elixir of Life in my bath, it immediately cured a friend's illness.'

'Your friend wouldn't be called Sloppy Botty by any chance?'

'Yeah, and he's a dolphin, a farting dolphin.'

'Oh Jonny, this is why I adore you so much; who could make up such amazing stories but you? Listen, I have to go now; my Dad's waiting.'

'Ok, see you tomorrow then.'

'Love you, Jonny, and your crazy mind.'

'Love you too, Isobel.'

* * * * * * *

Jonny slowly and effortlessly slithered into the ever-so-warm and strangely caressing hot water.

'How's Stroppy Botty today, Wall Eyed?'

'Oh, still sulking, eating everything rotten and stinky he can find, just hoping to be able to fart again.'

'Well, I am not about to change it, or would you prefer if I did?'

'NO,' all the sea life shouted as one.

'Yes, I would,' Stroppy Botty said quietly, adding, 'How about allowing me to blow bubbles that don't smell?'

'On the top of your silly head, Stroppy Botty is a hole; it's called a blowhole and a blowhole for an excellent reason. Can you guess what this blowhole is for?'

'I have a hole in my head? Well, I never knew that; wow, a hole in my head; who'd have thought? Why have I got a hole in my head?'

'So, you can breathe.'

'But you haven't got a hole in the top of your head, Jonny,'

'Yes, that's because I am a human, plus I don't live in the sea.'

Stroppy Botty then casually swam over to Oink, Jube, Faraway and Blue Sky One Eye, who has now got a new name, Blue Sky Two Eyes, and ever so casually took a look.

'Good grief, well I never, who'd have thought, god bless my soul, they all have holes in their heads,'

'Yes, Stroppy Botty, they do, and would you like to know why?'

'Err, yes, please,'

'BECAUSE WE'RE ALL DOLPHINS, LIKE YOU.' Oink, Jube, Faraway and Blue Sky Two Eyes all shouted back.

'I'm a dolphin? I feel a song coming on.'

'I'm a dolphin?
I'm all-singing

Dolphin dancing
Tail flapping
Stinky frapping
Toe-curling
Nose holding
Bubble making
Parpy baking
Bra wearing
Joke sharing
Lost my bearings
and my earrings
Plus my hearing
Cornish fairings
Friends for sharing
Panty tearing
Botty parping, dolphin.'

Then, with perfect timing, Stroppy Botty blew hard through his blowhole, which sounded just like a fart.

'I got my parping back,' Stroppy Botty shouted with utter delight as he swam up and down merrily, making parping noises through his blowhole or parp-hole.

Jonny swam down through the crystal-clear water, leaving Stroppy Botty to his own devices, and sat in front of the golden globe.

'Jonny, there is danger coming,' Cheroo whispered.

'Who this time?'

'Rabid Rectum is coming, and he wants the elixir of life.'

'Yes, I am sure every greedy, selfish, self-absorbed, egoistic, evil entity in the multiverse wants it, but they're not going to get it.'

'Jonny, bring your friend and let her bathe in this water.'

'You mean Gracie? How do you know about Gracie?'

'Yes, bring Gracie, and then create your machine for the good of humanity.'

'Yes, Mother, I will. I love you, Mother.'

'I love you more, Son.' Jonny swam up to the surface and, in one well-practised leap, jumped clean out of the bath, landing perfectly in his slippers.

'Jonny, why don't you make a swimming pool?' Legend asked.

'Then fill the pool with the lifesaving waters, like Jala.'

'Yes, that's a great idea, but I will need to get the Professor's help as I have no idea what I am doing.'

'Well, not for the first time, eh Jonny,' Legion quipped.

'Hidden in plain sight,' Jonny replied, ignoring Legion's silly words.

'Wouldn't have to be huge, perhaps like a small plunge pool,' Legend added.

'Yes, a small pool in front of a large pool? Mmmmm that makes sense,' Jonny replied as he, Legend, and Legion ran up the old wooden stairs to his bedroom. Jonny checked under his bed to ensure all the parts were still there.

'I really should try and find a better hiding place,' Jonny said out loud.

'Jonny, if the place where the Elixir is right now is the safest place ever, then why move it?' Legion asked, showing an unusual amount of intelligence.

'Good point, Legion. Wasn't that a good point, Legend?'

'Well, it was a point. Unsure if it was that good.'

'Well, it was a point. Unsure if it was a good one,' Legion replied childishly.

'I wonder what would happen if we moved the bath?' Jonny asked, adding, 'I think there is something extraordinary about where it is, don't you? I mean, wasn't it somehow connected to Stonehenge?'

'Ley Lines?' Legion asked.

'Yes, there is certainly a connection here, but I don't understand that Ley Lines run under the ground, not thirty-odd feet in the air, and an old bathtub.'

'Maybe there are Ley Lines above ground, and no one's noticed,' Legion added.

'Like an extra-terrestrial highway?' Legend said, then added, 'I wonder what was here before this house?'

'Yeah, good point. I mean, there are chalk mines under us. I will ask Dad later. Let's ask him now. Race you downstairs.' In an instant, Jonny disappeared, reappearing at the bottom of the stairs, followed seconds later by Legend and Legion.

'Took your time, boys,' Jonny said, smiling.

'Yes, it seems we forgot about the flying invisibly bit.'

'Dad, do you know what was here before this house was built?'

'No idea, Son, but if you go to the local library, they will have documents.'

In a flash, Jonny, Legend, and Legion arrived inside the now-closed Little Plopping library.

'Right, where are the maps?' Jonny whispered.

'Jonny, you don't have to whisper, the library's closed, remember?'

'Oh yes, silly me.'

'Found them,' Legend shouted, his deep voice echoing around the old, hardly ever-used library.

'Blimey, these are old,' Jonny said, blowing the dust off the old parchments. Jonny carefully laid out map after map and quickly noticed nothing was mentioned about where his home was situated, nor was anything written about local chalk mines.

'Why don't we go and take a look?' Legion suggested.

'Oh yes, let's do that,' Legend added.

'Ok, why not? Let's go now, after three. One, two, thr...'

In a flash, all three disappeared from the musty, cobweb-hanging, damp-smelling old library and reappeared in the chalk mines' entrance.

'God, I forgot all about this,' Jonny said as he stood open-mouthed.

'It's still stunning, isn't it?' Legend added.

'It's all grown, but who has been looking after it all this time? How long has it been since we battled with Deadsheda and Dances with Death?' Jonny asked while still taking in the utter beauty of the disused mines.

'We need to go further, perhaps further down,' Legion suggested.

'Listen, it's getting late. Let's check it out tomorrow after school.'

'Ok, Jonny, great idea. Race you ba...' But Jonny had vanished before Legend could finish his sentence.

'Such a show-off,' Legend said to Legion.

'I heard that,' Jonny replied.

* * * * * * *

The very next day, Jonny, Legend, and Legion went back to the caves, but this time, they got in through the kitchen entrance. Armed with nothing but a torch, they descended at a pace down the old, slippery stone stairs that seemed to go on forever.

'What's that you're looking at, Legend?'

'I think it's an old door, Jonny.' Jonny shone his powerful torch towards where Legend and Legion were both busily sniffing the ground.

'Smell anything of interest, boys?'

'Just damp,' Legion replied.

'Ok, mind out of the way,' Jonny said as he kicked hard against the old door.

'My God, did you hear that? The door groaned,' Legion said in astonishment.

'Well, so would you if you got kicked that hard,' Legend replied.

'Do it again, Jonny.'

'No, no, please don't. I will let you enter if you tell me the password,' the door said gently.

'Jonny, the door's speaking,' both Legend and Legion said in unison.

'Yes, I heard, but what password?' Jonny replied.

'Jonny, the door just spoke; doesn't that seem strange?' Legend asked while pointing at the old door.

'Yes, I suppose it does. Hold on, I'll ask its name. Hello, old door, my name is Jonny, and these are my...'

'...two loyal friends, Legend and Legion,' the door replied nonchalantly.

'What, how on earth did he...' Legend asked in surprise.

'I might be a she,' the door butted in again.

'Ok, then how on earth did "THE DOOR" know that?' Legend asked again.

'I have forgotten more than you know, young Nerrac.'

'The door knows your true identity, Nerrac; how is this possible?' Jonny said, astounded.

'What is the password, Jonny?' the door asked.

'I don't know.'

'Yes, you do. You don't know that you know, but you do know, believe me, you know.'

'No, I don't.'

'Yes, you do.'

'Willy wobbles,' Jonny said, laughing. 'Very close, Jonny.'

'Really?'

'No, nowhere near.'

'Pssssst, Jonny, try the Lord's Prayer,' Legend whispered.

'Our Father...'

'In Aramaic, Jonny,' Legion butted in.

'Abwun

(Oh thou, from whom the breath of life comes)

'D'bwaschmaja

(Who fills all realms of sound, light and vibration)

'Nethkadasch Schmach

(May your light be experienced in my utmost holiest)

'Tete Malkuthach

(Your heavenly domain approaches)

'Nehwe tzevjanach asemenea d'bwaschmaja af b'arha

(Let your will come true in the universe-all that vibrates; Just as on Earth-that is material and dense)

'Hawvlan Lachman d'sunkanan jaomana

(Give us wisdom, understanding, and assistance for our daily needs)

'Wasc boklan chauben wachtahen asemenea daf chnanschwokeni'chaijaben

(Detach the fetters of faults that bind us and 'karma' like we let go of the guilt of others)

'Wela tachlan i'nesjuna

(Let us not be lost in superficial things, materialism, everyday temptations)

'Ela patzan min bischa

(But let us be freed from that which keeps us from our true purpose)

'Metol dilachie malkutha wahaila wateschbuchta i'ahlamalmin

(From you comes the all-working will, the lively strength to act, the song that beautifies all and renews itself from age to age)

Amen.'

(Sealed in trust, faith, and truth, I confirm with my entire being).

'Excellent, Jonny, but that wasn't it,' the door replied.

'What, you made me recite the Lord's Prayer in Aramaic, then tell me it's wrong?'

'Yes, that's correct, but I didn't make you; you just did it. Blame her.'

'Who?'

'Her, Legion?'

'Yes, her.'

'Legion isn't a girl.'

'Looks like one.'

'Wee on him, it, err, her, Legion,' Legend said, laughing.

'Jonny, it's one word,' the door said gently.

Jonny sat down on the damp earth, put his head into his hands, and thought.

'What are you doing, Jonny?' Legend asked.

'Thinking,' Jonny replied, then shouted, 'It's one word.'

'Yes, that's what the door said, Jonny,' Legend said, giggling.

'Correct Jonny, you may pass,' said the old door.

'Well, aren't you going to open then?' Jonny asked.

'Why would I? I am not the entrance; I am just an old door; there's the entrance over there.' Jonny spun around to see a set of old stone stairs going down.

'Well, thank you for your help, door,' Jonny growled.

'My pleasure,' the door replied, adding, 'Now can I go back to sleep?'

Jonny, Legend, and Legion walked down the old stone stairs and suddenly found themselves standing in front of Dentro Reclu, who, in turn, was standing by the lost city of Amaranta.

'Hello, Jonny, Legend, Legion,' Dentro Reclu said nonchalantly.

'Hello,' all three replied.

'Don't lose sight of the invisible doorway, will you,' Dentro Reclu said, pointing at nothing.

'Legion, stand by the invisible doorway,' Jonny asked.

'I can't.'

'Why on earth not?'

'Because, as you said, it's invisible, so I can't see it.'

'It's ok, Legion, I will mark it for you,' Dentro Reclu said, throwing dust towards it.

'Why didn't you think of that, Jonny?' Legion asked.

'I'm still in shock, that's why. The last thing I expected was to be here.' Jonny then grabbed some dust and threw it at the invisible doorway. He tentatively poked his head through it, and right in front of him was the old chalk mine and a now sleeping, snoring door. Jonny pulled his head back, and again, he was standing next to a grinning Dentro Reclu and two baffled-looking dogs.

'This is incredible; no, this is more than incredible,' Jonny said in utter amazement, adding, 'You can get to Stonehenge via my old bath and to the Pyramids of Giza via the cellar.'

'Don't forget where you can get to from your bath, Jonny,' Legend whispered.

'Yes, right into the deepest oceans.'

'Your home, Jonny, is a crossroads to Ley Lines and a terrestrial highway. The earth's energy surfaces at several points around the earth, but nowhere is it more powerful than your home. I understand you spoke with an old door; is that correct, Jonny, an old door in the chalk mines?'

'Dentro, how on earth do you know all this? Even that old door knew about Legend and Legion being Nerrac?'

'Well, wake the door up when you return and ask him to open. You won't believe what's behind it, but be careful; he likes to play games.'

'Does he have a name?' Jonny asked.

'Open sesame,' Dentro Reclu replied, giggling.

'That was Ali Baba and the forty thieves,' Jonny replied quickly, adding, 'from the film One Thousand and One Nights, and it was used to open the mouth of a cave where the forty thieves had hidden their treasure. You're not telling me we should use the same silly made-up name, right?'

'Let's just say he has a funny sense of humour. Now you had better go, but now you know of this route, don't use it unless told. Do you understand, Jonny?'

'Yes, yes, of course, Dentro, I fully understand,' Jonny replied, picking up some dust and throwing it towards Legion.

'Jonny, try throwing the dust to my right and not right in my face if you don't mind,' Legion said, sneezing, coughing, and spluttering.

'Oops, sorry, Legion,' Jonny replied while picking up another handful of dust, missing Legion and finding the old invisible doorway. All three said goodbye to Dentro Reclu and walked single file through the invisible doorway.

'Having fun, are we?' the old door asked.

'Heart palpitations more like,' Jonny replied.

'Well, if you thought that was fun, wait to see what's behind me.'

'Don't tell me, Atlantis.'

'At where?' Legion asked. 'Atlantis,' the door replied.

'Yes, I heard you the first time, but what's Atlantis?'

'I'll tell you what Atlantis is. Atlantis is, you dim dog,' the door replied, adding, 'Not only does she look like a girl, but she is also as thick as my father.'

'Doors don't have fathers, you dim door,' Legion replied.

'What am I made of, dim dog, rubber?'

'No, you're made of stupid.'

'Mmmmm, you're calling me stupid, yet you have no idea what Atlantis is, plus you're a moron who looks like a very hairy girl.'

'Set fire to him, Legend,' Legion hissed.

'Ok, ok, let's have some calm here. So, door, do you have a name?' Jonny asked politely, trying to defuse the heated conversation.

'Yes, I do,' the door replied.

'Care to share?'

'Why don't you guess?'

'I know, it's Doreen, isn't it?' Legion said, almost wetting himself.

'It must be getting late; we should go,' Jonny said, trying to stifle his laughter but failing dismally.

'Bye Jonny, see you tomorrow, no doubt, but next time leave the sissy Mary one at home with her dolls,' the door said dryly and went back to sleep.

'Night, Doreen,' Legend and Legion replied, still giggling.

'Oh, and Jonny, don't forget Rabid Rectum the Effeminate is coming to steal the machine,' the door added.

'Is that his full name, Rabid Rectum the Effeminate?'

'Yep, it has a certain ring to it, don't you think?'

'A certain ring around it,' Legend said, laughing.

'Anyway, I haven't even started to build the machine yet,' Jonny added, surprised by the door's comment.

'You have been watched, Jonny, and been watched very closely. Trust only those you know and no one else.'

'Ok, door, will do. See you tomorrow, and I will discover what's hidden behind you.'

* * * * * * *

Jonny stepped out of the chilly chalk mine and into the kitchen's warmth, where he made himself a nice hot chocolate drink.

'Jonny, it's late. Where on earth have you been? We have been looking everywhere for you; it's way past your bedtime,' Lady Kathleen growled, adding, 'You're covered in dirt; take a bath immediately and then straight to bed.'

'Yes mum, sorry mum, it won't happen again, mum,' Jonny replied sheepishly.

Saturday soon arrived, and so did Gracie, who cycled independently, which was pretty impressive for a girl with a heart problem.

'I can't pretend, Gracie, but I got you here on false pretences,' Jonny said as he sat next to the little stream.

'Wow, you have beautiful dogs; what are their names?' Gracie said, completely ignoring Jonny's feeble attempts to be honest.

'Well, this one is called Legend, and this one is called Legion. Say hello to Gracie.'

'Ha ha, you're so funny; imagine dogs that can talk.'

'Yes, silly me, just imagine,' Jonny replied, smiling nervously as Legend and Legion shook their vast heads and put their considerable paws in front of their mouths as if to say 'shhhh.'

'I want you to, well, I know, err,' Jonny stammered, unsure how to tell Gracie about the hidden powers of his bathwater and running short of anything to say, he added, 'I know, let's kick the football about, and while you do that, you can tell me about your heart problems.'

Well, that seemed to work, as Gracie didn't stop for almost fifteen minutes, chatting vigorously about her 'Pediatric Cardiomyopathy.'

'I can help,' Jonny said bluntly.

'How can you help?'

'Do you trust me?'

'Yes.'

'This will sound odd, but I want you to bathe.'

'But I'm not dirty.'

'Would you take a bath if you were dirty?'

'Yes, of course.'

Jonny picked a handful of the mud from beside the stream and rubbed it in Gracie's face. Gracie ran over the muddy banks of the stream, got two handfuls of dirt, and threw them right into Jonny's face. Jonny wasn't expecting Gracie to have so much spirit, and immediately, a mud fight broke out. Within five minutes, they were both covered from head to toe with smelly mud.

'Now, will you take a bath?'

'Yes.'

'Ok, wait there, don't do anything; I will be back in a second,' and immediately vanished into thin air, leaving Gracie speechless.

'Ok, your bath awaits you; towels are on the door, and there's a clean jumper and my school tracksuit bottoms to wear. Now relax in the water and tell me how you feel, ok?'

'Ok, where do I go, and where did you go?'

'Legend, please show Gracie the bathroom.'

'Wow, your dog is so well trained.'

'Mmm, yes, sometimes.'

Gracie followed Legend up to the bathroom, where he sat and waited patiently outside the bathroom door as Jonny washed off the stinky mud in the stream.

'Do you reckon it will work, Legion?' Jonny asked while ducking his head in and out of the cold water, but before Legion could reply, screams were coming from the bathroom. Jonny and Legion vanished into thin air, arriving just in time to see Gracie emerge from the bath, clean, spotless and smelling less like stream mud.

'The...the...there's a dolphin in your bath, and he just farted,' Gracie said, stuttering hysterically.

'Yeah, erm, yes, he tends to do that. It used to be worse, but thanks to the refreshing water, he only farts through his blowhole and not his bum...'

'What, you mean you knew you had a farting dolphin in your bath, and you didn't tell me?' Gracie interrupted.

'How do you feel?'

'What, what, what do you mean, how do I feel? You have a...' Gracie stopped ranting for a second and then added, 'Actually, I feel great.'

'Better than you did before you got into the bath?'

'What, with a farting dolphin? Yes, yes, I feel fantastic,' Gracie interrupted, adding, 'my heart, it feels warm, it doesn't ache like it used to.'

In a flash, Gracie slammed the bathroom door, took off her clothes, and jumped straight back into the bath again, singing at the top of her voice.

'Think I preferred her before the bath, Jonny, less noisy,' Legend smiled, placing his enormous paws over his ears. Within minutes, Gracie emerged dressed and grinning from ear to ear.

'I must go home and tell my mum.'

'No, no, erm, not now, Gracie. It's a big secret, but to see if it's worked, can you go back and see your doctor, the heart specialist?'

'I already have an appointment on Monday, so yes, I can, and yes, I can keep a secret, Jonny, and I won't tell anyone what just happened.'

Gracie ran down the two flights of stairs and out through the kitchen door, and before she jumped on her bike, she ran around the entire perimeter of Jonny's garden, not just jogging, but at full sprint, giggling all the way, leaping and jumping like she had been reborn.

'I want whatever she's had,' Legend said to Legion, and in a flash of fur, both disappeared upstairs and jumped into the still-warm bath.

'Oh god, I hope they don't start singing,' Jonny whispered to himself.

Gracie finished running around the garden in what seemed only seconds, kissed Jonny full on the lips, got on her bike and pedalled away at breakneck speed, shouting, 'Love you, Jonny, thank you, Jonny,' and in an instant, she was gone.

'Jonny, don't forget the professor's coming over today,' Sir Ranulf said as he washed Genevieve, adding, 'Who was that in such a rush?' Jonny thought momentarily, remembering what Legend had said about these being 'simple people'.

'Oh, just that girl from school who wanted to talk tactics or something or other,' Jonny replied, quickly going upstairs to see what mayhem Legend and Legion had done to his bathroom. To his surprise, the bath was empty and clean, with no signs of a wet dog anywhere. Jonny ran up to his bedroom to remove the well-hidden artefacts that were cleverly hidden under his bed, and there, sitting on his bed, was Legend and Legion, who looked different. Jonny stopped to look at them, and they looked back.

'What are you doing?' Jonny asked, not taking his eyes off his two best friends.

'How do we look, Jonny?' they both asked.

'Younger,'

'Notice anything else?' Legend asked.

'You're on my bed, and you're both dry. You did jump into my bath, didn't you?'

'Leapt more like,' Legion replied.

'And?'

'Leapt, swam, dived, somersaulted, felt more alive than ever before,' Legend said.

'Breathe on me, Legend,' Jonny ordered, then asked Legion to do the same.

'Mmmmm, your breath doesn't smell of infested donkey plop, which is unusual as it usually does.' Legend then sniffed Jonny's breath, his armpits and feet, 'incredible, you don't smell like mouldy prunes.'

'Well, this must be a first, we don't stink,' Legend added.

'That must be one powerful medicine I have there if it can cure Gracie's heart and make you not only younger but also less smelly and stop Sloppy Botty parping for England. Well, imagine what the elixir can do on its own.'

'Then perhaps you already have the answer,' Legion said calmly.

'You mean, get sick and ill people to jump up and down in my bath; I don't think my parents will be too pleased.'

'No, Jonny dumb Plumb, I mean, use the bath water, not the bath. Take the water out of the bath; this way, no one can steal it.'

'Like a small bathing pool?'

'Yes, by jingo, I think she's got it,' Legend exclaimed.

'Then why do I have to build a machine then?'

'Mmmmm, he's got a point there, Legend, hasn't he, Legion?'

'Oh, poodle piddle, I thought I had the answer for a moment.'

'Hold on a moment; perhaps the water in my bath can cure only so much. Gracie's heart problem has to do with weak heart muscles; all the water has done is strengthen them, and as for us looking younger, well, that's just a stroke of luck. I need to chat with the Professor.'

Jonny sat with Professor Ziad in the kitchen and explained what had happened, how, and when.

'You know we said that all the parts of a clock by themselves are not much used, but together, they make it possible to tell the time.'

'Yes,' Jonny replied.

'Then we must build a huge clock.'

'Yes, in my bath?'

'Mmmmm, yes, see the problem there.'

'Not forgetting safety. I mean, this thing is worth trillions of billions.'

'Probably more,'

'Okay, then, a Googleplexian. Anyway, we know it has to be hidden. It has to be burglar-proof and...'

'What did you just say?' Professor Ziad butted in.

'Err, it has to be burglar-proof,'

'No, no before that,'

'That it has to be hidden?'

'No, before that.'

'Oh, err, the Googleplexian?'

'Yes, yes, what's that?'

'Oh, it's just the name for the biggest number. It's something like the number one with a million zeros after it, but to be honest, I am sure if you had time, you could keep adding zeros indefinitely. Anyway, let's err; build this machine, eh Professor.'

'Yes, yes, old cabbage, let's do that.'

* * * * * * *

Meanwhile, young Gracie underwent a series of tests and procedures at the Royal Brompton Hospital in London by the world-famous surgeon Doctor Richard Donkey.

'These results are just astonishing, Pauline; I can call you Pauline?' Doctor Donkey asked, scratching his bald head.

'Pauline is fine. So sorry, but my husband Frank couldn't be here today; he's away again on business.' Pauline replied, trying to stifle her laughter at the doctor's stupid name.

'Pauline, these results show that Gracie's heart is, well, erm, back to normal. In fact, better than normal. This is unheard of. I don't like to use this word as a professional doctor, but this is a God-given miracle.'

'A Jonny Plumb given miracle,' Gracie whispered, but she was overheard wrongly by old big ears, Doctor Donkey.

'Who is Jolly Crumb?'

'Plumb.'

'Plumb Crumble?'

'Yes, that's his name, Jolly Plumb Crumble,' Gracie said, realising that she had almost given the game away.

'What a strange name.'

'Yeah, like you can talk, Doctor Donkey,' Gracie whispered.

'Well, Gracie, this is incredible, a miracle.' Gracie and Pauline skipped out of the Royal Brompton Hospital, beaming from ear to ear.

'So, Gracie, what did happen at Jonny's house then?'

'I will only tell you, Mummy, if you promise not to tell a soul, not even Dad?'

'I tell you what, Gracie; I don't want to know, as I am just the happiest mummy in the world. Let's have an ice cream, and then, what would you like to do?'

'I am going to be the greatest footballer, sorry, female footballer in the world.'

'Yes, Gracie, I think what you said first sounds better, right?'

'You mean the greatest footballer?'

'Yes, Gracie, the best.'

* * * * * * *

'So, Professor, these are the bits I have now. The other parts, well, not so easy to get at the moment, but what do you think?' Jonny asked as he laid down the thirteen singing rune stones, the single hair from Stump Grinding, a tear from Isobel, the rose petal from the Queen of Iceland, one very sharp shark's tooth, the bone ring, the Lord's Prayer written in Aramaic and the one hundred phials on top of Jonny's bed.

'What's missing then?' the Professor asked as he gazed at the weird assortment of objects on and under Jonny's bed.

'Ah well, err, the golden globe, a shard of pure light and, most importantly, the elixir of life.'

'Well, they seem to be the energy required to run this machine. Let's call it Beryl for the time being, but these other bits, well, it's quite a jigsaw, Jonny, and to be honest, I am completely flummoxed.'

'Flum what?'

'Flummoxed, Jonny. It means confused.'

'Well, that's two of us then, but I know this: I simply moved this elixir into my bath, which in turn made healing water.'

'Explain further.'

'Ok, well, err, I have a friend called Gracie, who has an incurable heart disease, which I think is called Pediatric Cardiomyopathy, and, well, she took a bath, well, two baths actually, and she felt...'

'Jonny and Pauline were on the phone. Gracie's mother and Gracie had been to see the heart specialist, Doctor Donkey, something or other, and she had been cured. I just thought I would pass the message on. Hello, Professor,' Lady Kathleen interrupted as she stood in the doorway of Jonny's bedroom.

'...Well, as I was saying, it seems that she has been cured, and that was just by taking a bath. I mean, two baths. I am not a heart specialist, Jonny, as well, you know, but to cure any heart disease just by soaking in a bath is quite unbelievable.'

'It can probably cure Philomena's bottom burps.'

'Really, you mean that, Jonny? Oh, that would be heaven, Jonny; I have put up with that woman's constant machine gun frapping for almost forty years. We have mushrooms growing from the ceilings, and we never have visitors. When can she come over?'

'Whenever, Professor, now if you want.'

'Right, I will get her straight away, back in three shakes.' While Jonny waited, a thought sprung into his mind. He was given a Meccano set last Christmas but forgot where he had put it.

'Oh, I know it's under the stairs,' Jonny mumbled and strolled down the stairs, followed by two exquisite-looking dogs that just had to stop and check out their reflections in the landing mirror. Jonny rummaged around the cobweb-strewn cupboard and finally found the never-used Meccano set. Jonny ran back up the two stairs to see Legend and Legion still preening themselves in the mirror.

'Oh, for God's sake, it's unimportant. I mean, how you look.' Jonny grumbled as he walked past. Jonny laid the box on the floor and started to take out the pieces, which included metal plates with holes in screws and bolts and began, in earnest, building a frame for the golden globe and the elixir of life hidden within.

'Crikey, that was quick,' Jonny said as Professor Ziad returned with his mad-as-a-bat-parping wife, Philomena, who had brought her swimming costume, swimming hat, goggles, flippers and snorkel.

'You're taking a bath, not swimming across the Channel,' Jonny said, laughing but was silenced by an actual nose curler of a parp. 'Best get her in there, Jonny, as soon as possible; I'm unsure if I can take another one.'

Jonny ran a bath and told the Sea Life that it might be an idea to swim to safety.

'Ok, Philomena, your bath awaits you,' Jonny said, bowing. Dressed in a flashy pink swimming costume, Philomena shuffled into the bathroom wearing her flippers, goggles, and snorkel. Jonny while Legend, Legion, and even the Professor were rolling around the floor in hysterics.

Five minutes passed with no sound when suddenly there was the loudest and longest parp known to man or beast. The bathroom door slowly opened and out walked Philomena, who had the biggest smile ever.

'Are you ok, my little parp bubble?' Professor Ziad asked.

'Oh, I feel wonderful, never better,' she said as she removed her flippers, goggles and snorkel.

'My God, Philomena, you look stunning,' Professor Ziad said in disbelief.

'I feel stunning,' Philomena replied as she gently wafted past the stunned, open-mouthed Professor and the amazed Jonny, Legend and Legion.

'You smell beautiful, you smell of roses, a garden of blooming roses,' Professor Ziad said, still suffering from mild shock.

'I am as beautiful as a garden of roses, my darling,' Philomena replied with grace and elegant posture. Without hesitation, the Professor dived headfirst and still fully clothed into the bath as Philomena got changed. Within minutes, he was singing at the top of his voice, 'I feel pretty, oh so pretty, I feel pretty and witty and gay.'

Within five minutes, the Professor emerged from the bathroom, wrapped in two towels and grinning from ear to ear.

'Horace, you look so handsome,' Philomena said, fully dressed and still smelling of roses.

'Horace?' Jonny said, giggling.

'Yes, old pancake, that's my name.'

'Well, I never knew that.'

'Jonny, whatever you have in that water is incredible; we must build this machine as soon as possible.'

'You know, Professor, perhaps we don't need to after all,' Jonny then imagined the long queues of people waiting their turn to take a bath in his bath, then said, 'Well, perhaps that wasn't such a wise idea after all.'

CHAPTER THREE:
EVIL RETURNS

'Jonny, you need to hear this,' Professor Ziad said as he turned the large volume dial on the radio.

'Reports coming in from NASA of unknown objects entering Earth's atmosphere. NASA spokesman Mr Phil Mypie says they are unsure if these are UFOs (unidentified flying objects), but there seem to be many. We will keep you posted.'

'Jonny, do you remember we said we wanted to thank you for everything you have done for my family?'

'Er, yes, Dad.'

'Well, it's your half-term next week, Jonny, so we're all going to Disneyland, and it's been arranged you can bring Isobel. Here, ring her up and tell her the good news,' Sir Ranulf said, passing Jonny the telephone. Jonny hurriedly dialled the number as Sir Ranulf turned the radio off.

'Hello Auntie McFaggot, could I speak to Isobel, please?'

'Och aye the noo, you could if she were here, wee man, but she is away in the hills, and it's not Auntie McFaggot, it's Auntie Haggis Itchysporan McPlop, but I can understand why you were mistaken. I will tell Isobel to ring when she returns,' Auntie Haggis Itchysporan McPlop said in her deep Scottish accent, and before Jonny could reply, the phone line went dead.

'Did you tell her, Jonny?' Sir Ranulf asked.

'No, apparently Isobel is away in the hills,' Jonny said, trying to imitate the broad Scottish accent but sounding more like an old Spanish goat.

'Well, Jonny, we booked a flight with BOAC for Monday. The bad news, old boy, is that if you want Legend and Legion to come, they must be medicated and kept with all the suitcases in the plane's hold.

'I do want Legend and Legion to come, but I won't allow them to be medicated, whatever that entails.'

'It means they have to be drugged as it's a very long flight.'

'Well, why don't we fly there in Rapture? We could be there in a second, plus the boys can come and not be drugged.'

'Didn't like to ask, old boy, as it wasn't my place.' Jonny then turned to Legend and Legion and whispered, 'But I don't know how to summon Rapture.'

Legend and Legion shook their enormous heads and shrugged as if to say, well, we don't know either.

'What about the Golden Globe?' Legend asked.

'It's got the Elixir of Life in it, so I can't use that. Tell you what, let's go and play in the chalk mines with your friend, the angry door and find out what is behind it.'

'Don't forget the torch,' Legion added as they all ran out of the lounge, through the kitchen, and down into the chilly chalk mines.

'Hello Jonny, come to see what's behind me?' the door said, yawning.

'Rather,' Jonny said excitedly.

'Do you remember the password?'

'Yes.'

'Well?'

'I am, thank you for asking.'

'No, dumb plumb, I wasn't asking if you are well because I couldn't care less; I was referring to the password.'

'Ooooo, who's got sand wedged in her keyhole?' Legion said in an effeminate voice.

'Oh God, you brought sissy Mary and her mother, and they've permed their hair, how sweet.'

'Door, how did you become so filled with anger?' Jonny asked.

'Oh, I don't know, perhaps being stuck down here for the past few million years hasn't helped my sense of humour.'

'Certainly screwed up your boyish looks and charm,' Legion replied, laughing.

'A million years? Did I hear you right, door? A million years?'

'Yes, Jonny, deaf aid, you heard me right. Right, sit down and Legion, take a hike while I tell you all a story. The earth on which this extraterrestrial house was built is the most sacred land. Have you ever looked closely at your home, what it's made of, how old it is, and why the windows never need cleaning or the paintwork redecorating? No, I thought not; the reason is what the house is made of, and nothing on earth comes close to it. Typical homes are built using bricks, stones, wood, and mortar; none exists in this house, or perhaps I should call it by its correct name, the ARC. No, not like Noah's old wooden boat or the Ark of the Covenant.

'Why here?' Legion added.

'Ah, she asks a good question, well, the reason is this. We are right now where the first alien spaceship landed and was huge. This huge spaceship, believed to be about one hundred miles wide, landed when the first signs of life began to form. Like Legion's brain, the simplest kinds of life, single-cell organisms called Archaea, thrived in hot springs next to volcanoes and beneath the vast oceans beside hydrothermal vents. The very first thing the aliens had to do was secure Earth, not to own, like land ownership is today, but only to set up a base. So, they sent pulse signals of incredible powers to encircle the earth just below the ground, also known as Ley Lines and just above it, called the Alien Highway. Once this was done, the alien race proceeded to help nurture Earth like a gardener cares for his garden. This race cared for earth.'

'What was this race of aliens called, and where were they from?' Legend asked.

'Well, this might be a bit of a shock to you, Jonny, but they came from Pashoo and were called The Pathens, and you, my young friend, are related to them. Welcome home.'

'So, is this house all the original spaceship then?'

'No, this house is built way above it, but the original spaceship still exists, but it's an awful long way down.'

'Ah,' Legion shouted out loud. 'Had a brain wave, trod on a tack, remembered your name?'

'No door, I have not, but I know what's behind you now. Is it the spaceship?'

'I take it all back; you are one smart dog, even though you look like your hair's been permed.'

'Is it really?' Jonny asked.

'What, her hair's been permed, or there's a huge spaceship behind it?'

'No,' the door replied.

'Err, the spaceship?'

'No,' the door replied, adding, 'the spaceship is here, but it's many miles below the ground and reaches fifty miles in each direction. The centre of the spaceship is directly below us, and your home, Jonny, is, in fact, part of this huge spaceship.'

'Why is it called the Ark?' Legend asked.

'Because, Legend, one day, in the not-too-distant future, all life on earth will cease to exist, and this spaceship, which brought and nurtured life, will also remove what little of it remains.'

'What? I don't believe this.'

'Sorry, Jonny, but it's true, not many civilisations survive, and fools too often and too easily lead humanity.'

'How much time have they got?' Legion asked tentatively.

'Well, Legion, first we must overcome greed, and we all know that the greediest, most selfish, self-loving entity is heading our way.'

'Rabid Rectum the Effeminate?' Legend whispered.

'Yes, the very same, and he wants two things: the Elixir of life to make himself perfect and for people to love him. And believe me, they will.

Like the Devil, he is only interested in himself, and no one else matters.

'Does he know the whereabouts of the Elixir?'

'No, Jonny, he does not, and he must never find out, which brings me to where to house it?'

'Here,' Legend, Legion and Jonny replied in unison.

'Yes, but all the important parts must be housed within the spaceship.'

'Yeah, makes perfect sense, plus it means I don't have to create a machine. That's right, isn't it?'

'Yes, you are correct, Jonny; the Ark has a special place ready and waiting. All you have to do is find the spaceship, which shouldn't be that difficult, then find the secret room and place all the sacred objects in this sacred room and seal it forever. One more question, Jonny: did you allow a certain girl into your bath to be healed? Is that correct?'

'Correct.'

'You must ensure that she has no memory of this, and you must do it soon, as Rabid will use her to find the Elixir.'

'But how could he know?' Legend asked. 'He doesn't, yet, but it wouldn't take long. Think about it: a local girl gets cured of fatal heart disease, a local girl who happens to go to the same school as Jonny.'

'Yes, you have a point,' Jonny replied.

'Right, Jonny, you must go now, and I must sleep, and you must come back tomorrow with all the sacred artefacts. Oh, and one more thing, Jonny, the spaceship?'

'Yes, what about the spaceship?'
'You will be flying it.'

* * * * * * *

The next day after school, Jonny gathered all the sacred and not-so-sacred objects and ran a hot bath.

'How's the parping, Sloppy?'

'Well, just listen to this.' Sloppy Botty said and then proceeded to play the Trumpet Voluntary perfectly through his blowhole. If that wasn't amazing enough, the rest of the Sea Life joined in.

'Well, I have seen and heard some incredible things in my short life, but I have never heard a dolphin do that.'

'Must be something in the water,' Squelch added. Jonny dived down to see the golden globe flashing, and in a well-practised move, he lifted it plus the shard of pure light and returned to the surface.'

'Going anywhere nice, Jonny?' SloppyBotty asked as he swam around the bath in ever faster circles.

'I have to build or, should I say, place all the objects I have collected into a spaceship, which is...'

'One hundred miles below us,' the entire sea life replied as one.

'Oh, you know about the spaceship then?'

'Know about it and heard about it,' Wall-Eyed Wally replied.

'You know, Jonny, that once you place all the sacred and not-so-sacred objects in the spaceship, you will never be able to fly in the silver flying arrow spaceship again?' Faraway whispered.

'Oh, no, I didn't know that. That's a real shame; I enjoyed flying around the universe in that,' Jonny replied mournfully.

'The fact that you're willing to give up so much to help others is incredible,' Stench added.

'It's not an easy choice,' Jonny replied ruefully, adding, 'but I guess it's one I must take.'

'You won't forget us, will you, Jonny?' Wall Eyed Wally asked while washing Jonny's hair.

'No, of course not; why would you even think that?'

'We were worried and concerned, that's all.'

'Well, be worried no more, as I am not going anywhere.' Jonny jumped out of the bath and carefully wrapped a towel around the Golden Globe and Shard of Pure Light as they flashed unique colours in unison.

'They know they're going home,' Faraway whispered.

Jonny quickly dried himself and ran up the old creaking stairs, followed as always by the ever-so-faithful Legend and Legion. As soon as he walked into the room, all hell broke loose as all the sacred and not-so-sacred objects lying on Jonny's bed suddenly flew unaided towards the Golden Globe, which ever so slowly enlarged. At the same time, it opened, allowing everything, including the one hundred phials, to fly silently in.

'Jonny, you're glowing,' Legend said, smiling.

'I feel... I feel...'

'With your hands?' Legion butted in, giggling.

'No, but I feel lighter like a great weight has been lifted from my shoulders.'

'Perhaps knowing the truth and not having to worry about things anymore, to enjoy life and relax a bit.'

'What truth?' Jonny asked.

'The truth is, Jonny, that you were prepared to put others first irrespective of your feelings and desires,' Legend said gently, adding, 'This is made even more difficult when you feel so alone in the world.'

'Yes, that is true, I do feel very alone, but in saying that, I am loved, aren't I?'

'Are you crazy, Jonny? What sort of question is that? Of course, you are loved.'

'Ok, race to the mines.'

* * * * * * *

'Hello, door.'

'Ah, hello, Jonny. It took me by surprise then. Oh my, what have you got there?'

'Sorry about that, door. Don't you have a name apart from "door"?'

'Yes, of course, I have a name, Essbeedee.'

'Essbeedee, hahaha, no, seriously, you have to be joking; no one in their right mind would call themselves Essbeedee,' Jonny replied, laughing his head off.

'What's so funny about my name then, Jonny?'

'Yes, Jonny, what is so funny about Essbeedee?' Legend asked, but Jonny couldn't reply as he was curled up on the dusty chalk floor in absolute hysterics while repeating, 'Essbeedee, Essbeedee.'

'Jonny, what is so funny about Essbeedee?'

'Silent but deadly, that's what's funny.'

'I don't understand, Legend. Do you understand this star child, who is as mad as a bag of broccoli?'

'No, Legion, I don't.'

'I do,' Essbeedee replied and began to howl with laughter.

'Well, would one of you morons be kind enough to explain, please?' Legend barked. Jonny drew three letters into the chalk dust, which were S-B-D.

'Ok, well done so that you can write three letters in the chalk dust,' Legion said, perplexed by the ongoing insanity.

Legend began to giggle, which soon turned into a bad case of hysterics.

'Silent but deadly,' he managed to utter before collapsing on the floor.

'Oh, laughing, isn't it wonderful? I mean, to laugh. I don't think I have laughed like that since, well, since I was a twig. So, ok, ok, where were we? Oh yes, I remember the sacred and not-so-sacred objects. You do understand where these objects originated, don't you?'

Jonny shook his head, 'originally? No, no idea, apart from where I got them from.'

'Well, each object, even Stump Grinding's huge whisker, has special powers. Isobel's tear has DNA, which, as you know, Jonny, means??'

'Did not attend,' Jonny replied, smirking.

'Try again.'

'Is it Deoxyribonucleic acid?'

'You're one smart kid, Jonny,' Legend said, smiling.

'The bone ring holds magical powers; the one hundred phials come from another place, another dimension, the Golden Globe? Well, what a creation. In short, all these sacred objects help give, protect and heal life, and when placed all together, they become the most potent object in the world, even more potent than love. When you eventually place them back into their rightful places, the Ark will continue to help heal the sick forever, and I mean forever. Now, Jonny, are you ready to fulfil your obligations and take these sacred objects home?'

'Err,'

'Good, then prepare for the fastest elevator in the world, going.........'

'Whoa, whoa, what do you mean going?' Jonny interrupted.

'...down.'

Suddenly, the floor where Jonny, Legend, and Legion were standing disappeared, and all three descended down a glass tube at an incredible rate of knots.

'We appear to be on a glass floor,' Jonny shouted at the top of his voice.

'Yes, two lumps, please,' Legend replied, unable to hear what Jonny was shouting.

'I have those in my pants,' Legion added, giggling. Jonny pointed at a pretend wristwatch while looking at Legend and Legion as if to ask, 'How much further?'

Legend and Legion shrugged their enormous shoulders as if to say, 'We don't have a clue.'

'Have we stopped? We seem to have stopped; I wonder if we have stopped?' Legend asked while walking around the glass floor.

'Certainly, very quiet,' Jonny replied.

'We seem to have been here for ages,' Legion added.

'The golden globe, it's floating all on its own,' Jonny paused for a moment before adding, 'like there's no gravity down here, wherever down here is.'

'Talking about where down here is, where is the lift out of here?' Legion asked, looking around, puzzled.

Jonny spun around and then around again; the dim, bluish light grew brighter and brighter.

'How do we get out?' Legend asked.

'How did we get in?' Legion added.

'What is this place?' Jonny asked as he began to explore his new surroundings.

'It looks like everything is,' Jonny paused again as he put his hand out to touch the solid-looking structure, and his hand passed right through it, 'whoa! I wasn't expecting that.'

Legend and Legion soon joined Jonny in touching everything that looked solid, but there wasn't one solid bit.

'Weird!' Legend muttered.

'Jonny, how are we going to get out?'

'I don't know, Legion.'

'Are we trapped?' Legend asked.

'No, of course not; remember, we can all disappear, can't we?' Jonny replied with a hint of fear in his young voice.

'Well then, let's get out of here,' Legion said, worried.

'Hold on, where has the golden globe gone?' Legend asked.

'Jonny, what's this?' Legend asked as he stood next to a very strange-looking object.

'Jonny, this place is full of religious artefacts,' Legion said as he walked around the vast, strangely lit and perfectly round room.

'Oh my God, what is this place?' Jonny added, almost passing out. Jonny paused momentarily, then asked, 'Did you feel that?'

'As in, did we feel something move?' Legend replied.

'Yes, I felt that as well,' Legion added before all three began to float.

'Why are we floating, Jonny?' Legend asked as he pretended to swim in mid-air.

'I have no idea,' Jonny said as he also began to swim, but being Jonny, he pretended to do the backstroke.

'This is fun,' Legion added while floating on his back in silence. Then, all three became artistic, making shapes, diving through pretend holes, and doing cartwheels like professional gymnasts.

* * * * * * *

'Nanny Carole walked into the lounge and, almost whispering, said, 'he's not in his bedroom, and his bed wasn't slept in last night,' to the worried friends and family who had gathered together and spent the entire night searching for Jonny.

'This isn't good,' Sir Ranulf said as he slowly paced up and down.

'Did you ring Eddie?' Charlie asked.

'Yes, old boy, the first person I called, and he has his men out searching, but there is simply no trace.'

'What about the cellar? Has anyone checked it?' Nanny Carole asked, then added. 'I know he had a bath last night because he didn't wash the bath as he usually does.'

'Nor hang up the towels,' Lady Kathleen said in a voice so quiet no one heard what she said.

'Did anyone hear the news last night? Well, the Vatican astrologists and all kinds of people believe that the devil's son has been born and that soon, whatever evil it is that's coming our way is almost upon us.'

'You don't think our Jonny has been taken?' Lady Kathleen asked, trembling.

Suddenly, the earth began to rumble, and the house started to shake as plates fell from the old Welsh cabinet in the kitchen with an almighty crash, making Philomena Flatulent Fudge-Bucket fart so loudly that it temporarily made everyone deaf. This old house's usually rock-solid foundations shook as more crockery smashed to the ground. Pictures began falling off the walls as if someone was throwing them onto the floor. The old grandfather clock began chiming even though it was only eight-thirty in the morning. Then suddenly, the entire house moved an incredible thirty feet into the air, moved by an incredible invisible force. Philomena Flatulent Fudge-Bucket continued to fart for humanity. Then, the roof tiles began crashing onto the ground, smashing into a thousand broken splinters. No one moved, not even an inch, scared witless by the earth-shuddering quake.

'What are you lot doing?'

Everybody spun round to see Jonny standing with Legend and Legion in the doorway.

'JONNY,' they all shouted as one, and then Lady Kathleen added, 'Where the hell have you been? We have been worried sick. ' She and the others rushed over to hug Jonny.

'I have some news for you, and I'm not sure you'll like it. So, if you would like to sit or stand, perhaps we should all sit. No, come to think of it, I am starving. So, can we please have some food and feed Legend and Legion?' Jonny blurted out. Nanny Carole ran off to the kitchen, and everyone quietly did as they were asked. They all sat down without saying a word, looking at each other as if waiting for someone to say something.

'Jonny, where on earth have you been? ' Sir Ranulf said we have been worried sick, breaking the eerie silence. He added, 'Charlie, ring Eddie and tell him to cancel the search.'

Within minutes, Legend and Legion had been fed and sat on each side of Jonny as Nanny Carole handed him a massive plate of chips and slices of bread, which Jonny quickly made into chip butties and devoured in seconds.

'Ok, right, well, I'm sorry, we disappeared, but we went down to the cellar with the Golden Globe to find the spaceship, you know, to put in all the bits that I have collected into a special room.'

'In a spaceship?' Sir Ranulf asked, unsure of what Jonny was talking about.

'Yes, Dad, in a spaceship.'

'A spaceship? In the cellar? Under our home?'

'Yes, Dad, in a spaceship, in the cellar, well actually, quite a bit lower than the cellar, but yes, under our home.'

'There's a spaceship under our home?' Lady Kathleen asked incredulously.

Suddenly, there was a knock, knock, knock at the front door.

'I'll get it,' Charlie said and quickly disappeared out of view.

'Yes, Mum, there is a spaceship under our home.'

'It's Isobel,' Charlie said as he returned to the lounge.

'Isobel, darling, what on earth are you doing here?' Lady Kathleen gushed as she beckoned to Isobel to come and sit down next to her.

'Jonny told me to be here.'

'I did?'

'Yes, you did.'

'No, I didn't,'

'Err, yes you did,'

'No, I didn't,'

'Jonny, why would I come from Scotland for no reason?

'But I didn't, I don't have a phone.'

'No, you are right, you didn't phone me.'

'See, I told you, I didn't tell you,'

'No, you told me you sent a message in my head.

'Isobel, you must come back immediately,' you said in my head.'

'Telepathy!' Professor Ziad said, knocking the old tobacco out of his old pipe, which frightened Philomena Flatulent Fudge Bucket into farting so loudly that the one remaining picture hanging on the wall dropped with a crash, which no one took a bit of notice of. Well, apart from Jonny, who stood up and looked at the remains of the pristine lounge.

'What the hell happened here?'

'We were hoping you might be able to tell us, Jonny,' Sir Ranulf replied.

Suddenly, there was another knock, knock, knock on the door.

'I'll get it,' Charlie said as he quickly disappeared out of view.

'It's your sister, Lady Kathleen.'

'I don't have a sister.'

'Well, this lady claims to be your sister.'

'My God, she looks just like you,' Professor Ziad said, looking up while filling his pipe with tobacco.

Lady Kathleen slowly stood up, mouth slightly open, staring in disbelief at the beautiful woman in the lounge doorway. Sir Ranulf also stood up, staring in disbelief, looking firstly at his wife and then at the woman who claimed to be his wife's sister.

'We were separated at birth,' the beautiful woman said in a voice that sounded the same as Lady Kathleen's, as one tear and then another slid almost in slow motion down the woman's pristine cheek. Lady Kathleen stood up with tears also welling up in her eyes. She gently tiptoed across the broken glass and antique vases that lay in smithereens scattered over the lounge carpet, and without really knowing what to say, she uttered, 'Sorry about the mess, my cleaning lady has gone on strike.'

Everyone howled with laughter as Lady Kathleen embraced her long-lost sister. Lady Kathleen's sister hadn't seen Jonny as he was sitting low on the pouffe, but Jonny couldn't take his eyes off this woman, and Legend and Legion hadn't taken their eyes off Jonny.

'It's his mother,' Legend mouthed to Legion precisely at the same time as Legion mouthed the exact words to Legend.

'Can I ask your name?' Sir Ranulf asked, still unable to take in what was happening.

'Yes, yes, of course, my name is Mary.'

'Erm, Mary, sorry, but why are you here?' Sir Ranulf asked nervously.

'Oh, that's easy, Jonny told me.'

'By telepathy?' Professor Ziad asked.

'No, by carrier pigeon,' both Lady Kathleen and Mary replied simultaneously and then burst out laughing.

Jonny stood up, still unable to take his tear-filled eyes away from this beautiful vision he had been waiting so long to see. Mary turned to look at Jonny and openly wept, 'My son, my son. Oh, my beautiful son.'

'Mother Mary,' Jonny yelled as he ran into his mother's arms.

'We need to talk,' Jonny said after a few moments as he led his two mothers to the sofa, where they sat beside each other, holding hands.

'Jonny, there is a dark force that has attached its evilness to you,' Mary said quietly and then asked, 'Have you built the Elixir yet?'

'How, how, how did you know about that?' Jonny stammered. 'That's not important right now, but when it's ready, you must be the first person to go into it, as we cannot leave until you have.'

'Leave, what do you mean to leave? You're not taking my boy anywhere,' Sir Ranulf said quite angrily.

'It's ok, Dad. I will explain. Has anyone looked out of the window recently?'

Charlie rushed to the front window and almost passed out at what he saw.

'We're floating,' he said, putting his reassuring, solid arms around Nanny Carole. Sir Ranulf and Professor Ziad rushed to the same window that an ashen-faced Charlie just looked through. They both looked at each other and whispered, 'he's right, we are floating.'

'Right, where were we? Oh yes, this house, well, Dad knows that parts of it have been built with alien technology and lies on a layline crossroads, but he doesn't know it is attached to a huge spaceship. This spaceship has been here for thousands of years, just patiently waiting.'

'Waiting for what, Jonny?' Nanny Carole asked tentatively.

'To take me home.'

'Ahem, to take all of us home,' Mary said, smiling.

'WHAT!!!' Sir Ranulf shouted in disbelief.

'She's right,' a familiar voice said from nowhere. Jonny knew immediately who it was, and there in all her glory was Nanny Noo and Stan. Mother Mary proceeded to pass out, and Philomena dropped an H-bomb of a parp.

'Hold on, can we all just sit down and Jonny, please explain what the hell is going on?' Sir

Ranulf said in exasperation, adding, 'I mean, even for me, this is just getting too strange.'

'Right, below us and attached to this home is an enormous spaceship, ready and patiently waiting to take us all home.'

'Is everyone going home? Wherever home is?' Nanny Carole asked. 'I'm not,' Isobel said quietly.

'What do you mean you're not coming home?' Jonny asked in absolute astonishment.

'I can't leave my mother, and I won't leave my mother. Anyway, where are you going?'

'Well, if I can finish my story. As I said, there is a humungous spaceship below us that we're attached to, and this spaceship has been hiding for thousands and thousands of years. We know great evil will soon take over the world, and we must leave soon.'

'How soon is soon?' Isobel asked.

'Hold on, let me tell you the rest of the story. Mary is right; I do carry a sickness, and if I stay here, it will not only kill me; it will also kill all of you. I have to become healed by entering The Elixir. The most important part is that we must leave and return only when it is safe. The destination of our journey is Pashoo, and we will leave tomorrow. So, Isobel, get your mother, and she can also enter the Elixir with me. We should all enter together, but once we have entered it, we cannot return to Earth until the evil has passed.'

'How long will that be, old boy?' Sir Ranulf asked.

'I don't know, maybe one or two years, perhaps longer. Dad, can you go with Isobel and find her parents so they can also come? The bad news is they are not immortals.'

'What, who are immortals?' Lady Kathleen said in utter disbelief.

'This is the sad part: only Legend, Legion, Mary, and I are, but I want you all to come back to Pashoo with me, to see the beauty of the universe and when the evil that is coming this way has been defeated, then you can come home, sadly you will all be a bit older.'

There was absolute silence until the deathly silence was interrupted by a giggling Lady Kathleen.

'No, I didn't think for one moment that Philomena was an immortal, nor that Isobel's mad as a bag of angry spinach mother was.'

'Jonny, I don't want to grow old while you stay young; I want to be immortal as well,' Isobel said while crying.

'I don't have the power to change you, or anyone else for that matter; don't you think I would if I could?'

'Isobel, we will be together forever if you want this. I know I do, but I cannot change the laws that govern our multiverse. Go and find your mother and father; bring them back here while the rest of us get ready for the journey of a lifetime.'

Isobel smiled as she wiped the tears from her pristine cheek and whispered, 'I love you, Jonny.'

'What on earth do we pack?' Nanny Carole asked.

'Toothbrush, after all, you will still need to clean your teeth,' Jonny replied, laughing.

'Is that all?' Philomena Flatulent Fudge-Bucket asked.

'I think Jonny was joking, my little parping princess,' Professor Ziad said as he, Philomena, Sir Ranulf and Isobel left to get their belongings and Isobel's parents.

While Jonny's mother gossiped, Legend, Legion and Jonny went outside next to the small stream. Apart from the broken roof tiles strewn across the lawn, nothing else had changed. Other than the garden, it was now floating and still attached to the humungous spaceship. Jonny took his sandals off and placed his little feet into the cold water, soon to be joined by Legend and Legion.

'What just happened?' shouted Grubb as he and his friends looked mournfully at Jonny and asked, 'Was that an earthquake? I thought we were all going to die.'

'No, Grubb, it wasn't an earthquake, though I would imagine it must have felt like one.'

'What's wrong, Jonny?' Grubb asked, as he could sense something was wrong.

'I have to leave soon and return to my planet. It might be good for you, your friends and your families to head for the large river where you will be safe.'

'Will you come back and visit me?' Grubb asked as he dived in and out of the water.

'Yes, of course I will. We leave tomorrow morning, so it might be best to head for the river sooner rather than later. The stream will, in time, return to normal, but there will be one difference: this house won't be here, but instead, buried deep below the earth, it will be an amazing machine and, above it, a lake with amazing healing powers. So, tell all your friends and get them to tell all their friends that if they ever get ill, all they have to do is swim in the pure waters.'

'Wow, thanks, Jonny. Bye, Jonny. We love you, Jonny. Rush back soon, Jonny.' Grubb shouted as he and all his friends began to swim towards the great river.

'Jonny, don't you find all this a bit difficult? I mean, saying goodbye to all you know?' Legend asked, then adding. 'I know I will.'

'Yeah, me too,' Legion added.

'It's been the greatest adventure ever. But it's not over. I mean, we will come back soon, won't we?'

'You know when we go back, it won't be anything like this, plus, yes, we will come back. We promised we would never leave you, and we never will. However, when we return to Pashoo, you understand that we will change back into Nerrac, but only for a short while.'

'I cannot imagine life without you two by my side,' Jonny said as he began to sob uncontrollably.

'We feel the same way, Jonny; we feel the same way.'

Jonny dried his eyes, hugged Legend and Legion and immediately burst out crying again. 'I don't want to go home; I want to stay here; I want to be here with you and my family and not have to run away to Pashoo. I'm not ready to leave yet.'

'Well, we don't have to leave, do we Legend?' Legion said quietly.

'No, we don't have to go, we don't have to do anything, and we can stay here and take on the biggest battle ever to happen on Earth. We have the Elixir in place; we can still fight for humanity;

the trouble is, Jonny, it's not our choice; it's yours...'

'Great, some choice,' Jonny replied without even looking up.

'Jonny, the news is on the television. I think you might want to see it,' Charlie shouted from the back door. With Legend and Legion at his side, Jonny got up, wiped the remains of his fear and sadness from his face and walked into the lounge.

* * * * * * *

'Nanny Noo, what, what are you doing here?' Jonny asked, his jaw almost hitting the floor with surprise.

'Hello, my lovely Jonny, how I have missed you and all my family; heaven's a wonderful place to be, but it's so lonely without you. So, Stan and I wanted to come with you all to Pashoo and then come back and live with you here when the wars are all over.'

'I don't understand this,' Jonny mumbled, adding, 'I didn't call you, or Isobel or Mother Mary.'

'Well, Jonny, there are things that none of us can explain. Can you explain love or that I did a balloon dance butt naked at my funeral? You did call, you called for help, and you called out to those who meant the most to you, and of course, we all came back for you. I know you don't want to go home to Pashoo, but we have no choice. We must accept what will happen and then return when it's over. Jonny, there is nothing you can do here to change anything, nothing at all.'

'Darling, where's Isobel's mother?' Lady Kathleen purred as Sir Ranulf, Isobel Philomena, and Professor Ziad returned laden with goodies.

'They won't allow her to leave,' Isobel sobbed.

'What do you mean they won't allow her to leave? She is not in a prison.' Lady Kathleen asked.

'A mental home, it is a prison, it has bars on the window, and she is stuck inside her cell all the time.'

'Bluebell, do you want your mother to come with us?' Jonny asked.

'Yes,'

'Then tonight we will get her,'

'You don't have the Golden Globe anymore, Jonny,' Legend whispered.

'You're right, but we do have the Arc, and don't forget that I can still do the old invisible trick, see.'

'You're still here.' Legend said smiling

'What about now?'

'Nope, still see you,'

'And now?'

'Nope, still see you.'

'What about now?' 'Jonny, you're about as invisible as a whale that's beached on the beach at Beachy Head in the holiday season that's singing a salty sea shanty.' Legend said, giggling.

'Crikey, that's never happened before.' Jonny said mournfully.

'You're losing your special powers, Jonny,' Legion added.

'That's another reason you must return to Pashoo, Jonny. Without your special powers, whatever it is that's heading this way will find you and capture you, and, well, I hate to think what it or they would do to you, but I can imagine it won't be singing your praise or bowing down in your honour.' Nanny Noo said gently.

'So how can we get Isobel's mother out of one of the most secure mental hospitals in the world?' Jonny whined.

'What about distraction?' Legend suggested.

'What! Distract the guards and staff with what, a song and dance routine while wearing gorilla outfits?'

'What a brilliant idea,' Professor Ziad added while removing a Gorilla outfit from one of the many bags he and Philomena had.

'I don't believe this,' Jonny said as Philomena removed one gorilla outfit from her suitcase and another. 'We wondered if these would ever come in handy,' she chortled.

'No, no, we will not dress up as Gorillas. It's wild, it's utter madness, it's a great idea, let's do it.' Jonny said, laughing.

'My Mother will die of a heart attack,' Isobel said, but could not stop herself from laughing as Professor Ziad and Philomena put on their gorilla suits and started running up and down like their bottoms were on fire.

'Oh, this is going to be fun,' Sir Ranulf said while wearing a gorilla outfit.

'I am not wearing a gorilla outfit, nor my sister,' Lady Kathleen said sternly.

'I am,' Mary replied while climbing into a gorilla outfit.

'I don't believe this,' Lady Kathleen said as she watched her closest friends, family, husband,

and two ghosts run around her lounge, which was still strewn with broken bits of her house while making gorilla noises as Legend and Legion rolled around the floor in absolute hysterics. Isobel stood motionless with her mouth wide open, unable to utter a sound.

Suddenly, there was a knock, knock, knock on the door.

'I'll get that,' shouted Charlie as he ran towards the front door in his gorilla costume.

'It's Pc Floppy; apparently, there have been reports of an earthquake in the area. Anyone hear this earthquake?' Everyone stood still while Pc Floppy walked into the lounge, unable to take in what he had witnessed.

'Wh, wha, what is happening? I mean, where are the Hunters,' Pc Floppy stammered.

'HERE, here we are, here, mad as a bag of spinach', they all shouted as one and continued running up and down the lounge, then over the furniture, tables and chairs while making noises like a group of insane gorillas.

'I was going to say there's an enormous spaceship under your home, and the drive to your home was ever so slightly steeper, almost vertical, but after this, I don't think I will mention it. Have you got any more gorilla costumes?'

'Yes, I just happen to have two more, one for you and one for Isobel's mother,' Professor Ziad said, passing PC Floppy the costume. He eagerly climbed into it and then began running around, making silly ape noises.

'Ok, let's make a plan to save Isobel's mother while we're all dressed up in gorilla outfits and barking mad.' Jonny said.

* * * * * * *

The group of garrulous gorillas and one, giggling with happiness, Isobel, all jumped into the Jungle Queen and set off to the lunatic asylum, also known as The Wacky Shacky. Soon, the Jungle Queen was merrily going, chug, bang, parp, as it wound its way around the winding lanes of Rutland on a beautiful sunny day, as all the inhabitants sang merrily at the tops of their voices.

Soon, the Jungle Queen arrived at the gates of the Wacky Shacky, and as planned, Isobel did her very best to explain this special surprise for her ill mother to the guards. There were 'um's and 'ah's and 'I'm not sure, by the over-officious officers on guard. Isobel began to sob, cry, and then wail like a deranged banshee; that seemed to have worked as the now embarrassed officers slowly lifted the barrier and let the group of garrulous gorillas drive in.

Slowly, they drove around to the back of the Wacky Shacky to where Isobel's mother was after dropping off Isobel by the main entrance. Where she whined, moaned and cried until she was allowed to see her mother. With keys jangling from the female officer's belt, Isobel marched towards her mother's cell at some pace.

'Just in time for her medication,' said the Matron who unlocked the vast locks on the cell door.

'Mrs. Taylor, you have a visi...,' but before the Matron could complete her sentence, she was silenced by Mrs Taylor, who was screaming and laughing about 'the group of gorillas dancing and a huge spaceship outside her window.'

'Yes, Mrs Taylor, it's OK. We know you're not well. I have brought you some stronger medication, and your daughter is here to see you.'

'Gorillas, dancing gorillas, spaceship,' Mrs Taylor repeated while pointing out the window.

'Now, Mrs Taylor, what have we told you about making up stories? I'm so sorry, Isobel, but this is how she spends her days; she thinks she felt an earthquake the other day. Phew, completely barking.'

'Look, two of the gorillas are floating in the air,' Isobel said as she pointed out the window.

'Oh, dear, not you as well,' the Matron said while measuring out the medication for Isobel's mother.

'Look, Matron. I know you don't believe me, but look,' Isobel pointed.

'Oh, OK, if you want to play this silly game. OK, let's have a l-o-o-k-o-u-t-o-f-t-h-e-w-i-n-d-o-w.'

The Matron peered out of the window, and sure enough, a group of gorillas danced outside the window, two floating and right behind them, filling the sky, an enormous spaceship. The Matron rubbed her eyes and then carefully peered out the window again. She then looked at the bottle of medication. She drank the entire bottle before jumping onto Isobel's Mother's bed, covering her head with the blankets while shouting, 'Floating, dancing gorillas, huge spaceships, floating spaceships and gorillas. I want my mum.'

Silently, Isobel expertly undid the window locks and gently slid the window wide open.

Without a moment to spare, Isobel and her mother were carried out of the window. Then all the gorillas, Isobel and her giggling mother jumped back into the Jungle Queen and quickly drove back to the main gate. All waved at the officer and drove off down the road. Giggling incredibly, they all went back through the leafy lanes of Rutland back towards home. Sadly, the alarm had been sounded, and within minutes, the Jungle Queen had been stopped by the correctional officers.

'Now then, now then, now then, what have we got here? Who's in charge?' the Guard asked.

Nanny Noo and Stan got out of the Jungle Queen, still dressed as gorillas, and waved to the prison officer in charge.

'I am arresting you for the kidnapping of one prisoner, I mean patient. You do not have to say anything, but anything you do say will be taken down and given as evidence against you. Is that clear?'

Both Nanny Noo and Stan nodded in agreement.

'The rest of you can go home or to the zoo or up a tree,' the officer said laughing, then added, 'By the way, which of you is Mrs Taylor?'

Nanny Noo waved frantically and, in a silly high-pitched voice, said, 'I am.'

Knowing that both Nanny Noo and Stan were more than a match for the simpleton in the uniform, they all drove off giggling like children.

'OK, let's follow them,' Jonny said, laughing as they followed the prison officer's van back to Wacky Shacky and hid around the corner.

Nanny Noo and Stan were then taken into the interrogation room, still wearing their gorilla costumes.

'Before we call the police, we just wanted to know why you kidnapped one of our special needs patients?' the officer asked while pacing up and down. Both Nanny Noo and Stan shrugged their shoulders and then began giggling.

'Matron, where's the Matron?' the officer asked, ordering one of the orderlies to 'go and find her.'

'She is hiding in Mrs Taylor's bed, sucking her thumb, and then shouting out about flying gorillas and a spaceship,' the orderly said breathlessly.

'Flying gorillas and spaceships? I don't believe it,' the officer said when suddenly both Nanny Noo and Stan began to float and then fly around the office, faster and faster, while the officer quivered with fright. Beyond frightened by the sight of the two flying gorillas, the orderly ran out of the hospital and down the road while screaming, 'Flying gorillas, flying gorillas,' and bumped straight into ten gorillas dancing in the road and fainted on the spot.

Meanwhile, Nanny Noo and Stan had vacated their gorilla suits and floated unseen towards the still cowering officer, slapped him several times before flying out of the door, and then vanished down the road.

By now, the alarm had been sounded, and all the Wacky Shacky security guards rushed into the officer's office to see him still cowering in the corner while repeating 'flying gorillas, flying gorillas' as he pointed to the two gorilla costumes still sitting in the chair. Without hesitation, two burly guards jumped into the now empty gorilla suits, knocking each other out.

* * * * * * *

'I need a bath,' Jonny shouted as he, Legend and Legion ran up the two flights of stairs to run a bath and explain to all his Sea Life friends what was about to happen. He stood while filling the tub, hoping beyond hope that he wouldn't have to lose such brilliant, funny and unique friends. Jonny jumped in with an almighty splash and washed his hair when all the Sea Life suddenly gathered around him.

'We all heard the earthquake, Jonny. Is it time for us to leave, to say goodbye to our best friend?' a very solemn Sloppy Botty asked.

'Well, erm, I think that, erm maybe, we have two choices,' Jonny replied, adding, 'one, you can all come back to Pashoo with me and then return here or wherever we come back to. Or two, I can set you free, back into the vast oceans with all your other friends.'

'You are coming back then, Jonny?' Carcass asked while climbing onto Jonny's head to help wash Jonny's hair.

'When the war is over, yes, I think so.'

'What war?' the Sea Life asked as one.

'Oh, some evil forces are heading this way, and I must return to Pashoo. Well, my family and I were wondering if...'

'...YES!'

'Yes, yes, what? I hadn't finished what I was about to say.'

'Yes, we all want to return to Pashoo with you.'

'Oh really? Are you sure?'

'Yes, I can't wait,' Squelch said, adding, 'When do we leave?'

'I am unsure, but it's sometime tomorrow.'

'That's a good time,'

'What is?'

'Sometime tomorrow, that's a good time.'

'Then tomorrow it is. Will you all be ok until we get to Pashoo, our journey's end?'

'Erm, we're flying to Pashoo in a bathtub?' Sloppy Botty asked.

'Yes, you and my family will fly through space in this tub. Sloppy Botty, we're all flying to Pashoo in a ginormous, humungous and gargantuan spaceship, and it just happens that this house is attached to it. Oh, that reminds me, I had better prepare the Elixir when we leave, as we all must enter it.'

'Why is that?' Wall Eyed Wally asked.

'We all have to go into it; firstly, to heal our bodies of all diseases, but most importantly, we can't go to Pashoo dirty as Pashoo is heaven. Plus, I will be getting all my special powers back.'

'Special powers!! Jonny, you're so funny, special powers; you don't have any special powers.'

'Yes, I do,'

'Ok then, special powers, Jonny, prove it.'

Jonny lay motionless as it suddenly dawned on him that he was now just another ordinary kid and not a kid who could vanish into thin air, have the intelligence of Einstein or have superhuman strength.

'I can still talk to you, can't I? Sloppy, Wall-Eyed Wally, Squelch,' Jonny shouted as he suddenly realised, he was alone in his bath.

'Legend, Legion, where are you?' Jonny shouted.

'Right here, Jonny,' both Legend and Legion replied.

'Oh, thank heavens. Oh, for an awful, frightening moment, I thought I had lost you.'

'On Earth, Jonny, we are your constant companions, but as you are more than aware, on Pashoo, we are Nerrac,' Legend replied as Jonny climbed out of the bath.

'Yes, I understand,' Jonny said as he dried himself, adding wearily, 'Let's go to bed.'

Jonny jumped into bed as both Legend and Legion lay down beside him. Jonny grabbed Pod and, as he had done for so many years and whispered, 'Night Legend, Night Legion. I love you more than life.'

'Night, Jonny, we already know. 'Legend and Legion replied in unison.

* * * * * * *

'Last day on Planet Earth,' Jonny said with a wry smile as he climbed wearily out of his warm bed, adding, 'Are you two sleepyheads ready?'

'Yes,' Legend said while yawning and stretching out his vast, sleek body.

'Yes, good morning,' Legion replied.

'Morning Legion, morning Legend, this is certainly a strange feeling. I feel like I should be going to school in that clapped-out, rust bucket of a school bus and being shouted at by those dim thugs.'

'Sounds like you're having second thoughts about leaving,' Legend said as he licked Legion's face.

'I am. I don't want to go, but I know I must.'

'But Jonny, you're a one-off; no one is like you or ever will be anything like you. What's the problem with that?'

'Well, just about everything. I want to be a normal kid who goes to school, is average at sports, sings out of tune, gets spots, has smelly feet...'

... 'Oh, you have them alright,' Legend interrupted Jonny mid-rant.

He has an everyday life, takes exams and fails, gets cold in summer and turns red when a girl looks at him. Yeah, I want to be normal.'

'Do you wish you had not been born then, Jonny?' Legion said, smiling.

'Phew, that's a hard question to answer, Legion.'

'Well, okay, then, let's make it easier for you. Let's begin by taking away everything you have, starting with...' Legend paused for a moment and then, looking Jonny straight in the eyes, softly said, 'us.'

Jonny thought momentarily, then whispered, 'You're right, I should be grateful, shouldn't I?'

'Yes,' both Legend and Legion replied.

'Right, wash, then breakfast, then I need to get the Elixir up and running and then, well, we all jump into the spaceship and then go, I guess.'

Jonny ran downstairs to wash his face and teeth and then peered into the empty bath.

'Don't worry, Jonny; you will see them again soon.' Legend said, adding, 'This isn't an end to life, Jonny; it's just the start of another one. You're getting older now, and life changes as you grow older.'

'I know Legend; it's just that I don't want it to change. I loved life, and now everything is out of control, and I wouldn't say I like it.

'Listen, let's go and fix up the Elixir and then have a chat, ok?' Legion said gently.

* * * * * * *

Everybody seemed very quiet as they quietly rushed around, picking up things they thought they might need in Pashoo and putting them straight back. There was a kind of melancholy, a sadness to be leaving. Jonny walked down to the old cellar with Legend and Legion, still expecting the old cellar to be there, but it wasn't there anymore; instead, there was a massive hole in the ground. Jonny, Legend and Legion carefully peered into the abyss to see a fluorescent blue light and a vast pool of what looked like water right at the bottom of this enormous hole. Suddenly, and without warning, the fluorescent blue water began to rise at an astonishing rate, stopping just inches from the top.

'Weird,' Jonny said quietly as he touched the water.

'Whoa, that feels odd. It's warm, but it's cold, it's wet, but it's dry.' Jonny picked up an old bucket and tried to fill it. The weird water immediately vanished. He then tried to wash his face by making a cup shape out of his hands, and again, the odd water just evaporated before his eyes.

'It won't allow me to take it away. It seems to have intelligence; it's smart water.'

'It's not going to allow anyone to steal it, Jonny, now that's clever,' Legend said while peering into the perfectly crystal-clear water.

'It's bottomless,' Legion sighed.

'What, it hasn't got a bottom?' Jonny said, laughing as he peered deep into the abyss again.

'Jump in, Jonny,' Legend said gently. Jonny slipped off his slippers, removed his socks, shorts, and jumper, and tentatively placed one foot into the water.

'Wow, it's holding my weight,' Jonny shrieked excitedly as he carefully placed his other foot into the water, half expecting to sink quickly. He didn't.

'Now, try walking across it,' Legend said.

Jonny took one tentative step and then another and then another.

'It's liquid, but it's solid,' Jonny whispered, and then, without warning, he screamed as he suddenly sank, stopping just before his nose went under the strange water.

'You screamed like a sissy,' Legend said, laughing.

'No, I didn't; I was frightened, that's all.'

'No, Jonny, Legend was right; you did scream like a pansy in peril.'

'Ok, so if you're both so brave, come in and join me.' Jonny said as he relaxed back into the weird water.

'Hey, you know the invisible but most comfortable seats in the world, where they wrap around you when you sit in them? Well, this feels the same. Weird water, huh? Well, what are you two waiting for, swimming costumes?'

Without prior warning, Legend just leapt in, soon followed by Legion and half expecting to get splashed; Jonny was amazed to see that there wasn't a single drop or ripple.

'Wow, this feels so gooooooooooooooooooooooooooood,' Legend said, almost purring with pleasure.

'It sure does, Legend. I mean, this is just wonderful,' Legion replied, resting on his back with his four legs sticking straight out of the water.

'How do you feel, Jonny?' Legion asked.

'Without a care in the world, I feel so alive.'

'Special powers returned Jonny?' Legend asked as he lay sprawled out in the ridiculously relaxing water.

'Did I just disappear?'

'Yes.'

'Result,' Jonny said, punching the air, adding, 'Perhaps we should get everyone else to come in.'

'Yeah, I think you are right,' Legend said as he gently climbed out of the pool of weird water.

'Whoa,'

'What's wrong, Legend?' Jonny asked.

'Nothing's wrong, Jonny, everything is right, and I am totally dry.'

'And your coat, wow, it's incredible. Legend, you are shining.'

'I am?'

'You are.' Legion then paddled through the weird water and effortlessly climbed out of the pool of bizarre water.

'How do I look?' Legion asked.

'Oh, just the same old flea-bitten mutt,' Jonny said, laughing.

'What! How come Legend looks beautiful, and I don't?'

'I'm just joking; you look as beautiful as Legend,' Jonny replied.

'No, he doesn't; nobody looks as ravishing as me.' Legend said as he pranced up and down, his massive head held high. Jonny then also climbed out of the water, feeling incredible.

'This is something else; how can we hide this when we leave?'

'I am certain it has its way of protecting itself, apart from the fact that you can't carry it, drink it or even remove it.' Legend said, staring down into the vast pool.

'Ok, let's get all the family.' Jonny said excitedly.

'Everybody, come here now,' Jonny shouted as he ran back through the kitchen and into the lounge.

'What's the matter, old boy? Are your pants on fire?' Sir Ranulf replied, smiling.

Without replying, Jonny grabbed his father's huge, gnarled hand and dragged him back through the kitchen and down into the cellar, quickly followed by everyone else.

'Hey Nanny Noo, Stan, you try it as well.' Jonny enthused.

Suddenly, Jonny's entire family had all stripped to their underwear, apart from Nanny Noo and Stan, and fearlessly jumped in and immediately sank up to their noses as Jonny had done before.

'How does it feel? Great, isn't it?' Jonny said, beaming from ear to ear.

'It's just incredible; I feel like all the troubles of my entire life have just vanished.' Lady Kathleen said, relaxing in the weird water. Everyone was so wrapped up in the life-changing waters that no one had noticed what was happening to Nanny Noo and Stan. No one had noticed that they were changing back to mortals.

'Oh my God,' Jonny shouted, as he was the first one to notice that Nanny Noo and Stan were not only alive and human, but they looked younger, a lot younger.

'My God, it can bring the dead back to life,' Professor Ziad said in amazement.

'Ok, before you all run off to the graveyard to dig up your old relatives,' Jonny said laughing, 'I do think that this is a one-off, isn't that right, Nanny Noo?'

'Sadly, we're still dead, but we have decided to stay here and protect this place until you return. You can see us as we are, but no one else can.

'Can you hear banging?' Jonny asked.

'It's ok, I'll get it,' Nanny Noo said as she floated back through the kitchen and hall to open the front door.

'Hello, is there anyone at home?' Sir Harry Pinner asked as he and his wife Bunty peered around the now wide-open front door. Without wanting to alarm them, Nanny Noo quickly floated unseen back to the cellar and told them they had visitors.

'You never told me you had built a swimming pool, old boy,' Sir Harry asked, staring in disbelief at the goings-on.

'You never asked me, old boy,' Sir Ranulf replied.

'Did you build it while we were away, old boy?'

'No, no, old boy, Jonny discovered it. I mean, built it.'

'And what's with that bally great spaceship, old boy? Did Jonny build that as well?'

'No, definitely not, old boy. Tell you what, get down to your undies and jump in.'

'What, in there, old boy, with all you lot?'

Sir Harry and Lady Pinner immediately stripped off and leapt in.

'Tallyho, old boy,' Sir Harry shouted and immediately sank to his nostrils.

'This is funny stuff, isn't it, old chap?'

'Yes, it is a rather old boy. By the way, do you have anything planned for the next few weeks, maybe a month?'

'Nope, absolutely nothing, have we, darling?'

'No darling, absolutely nothing,' Lady Pinner replied. 'Good, then, well perhaps Jonny would like to tell you where we're all going.'

'Disneyland, old boy?'

'Better than that, old chap.'

'What, better than Disneyland, Cripes? Where could that be?'

'Try outer space,' Lady Kathleen said, smiling.

'What, in that giant spaceship outside?'

'Yes, that's the ticket, but we're in it now.'

'Not for long,' Jonny said, adding, 'I think it's time to get out of the pool.'

Everybody climbed out and, for no apparent reason, immediately began laughing and laughing.

'Never felt this well in my entire life, old boy,' Sir Harry said between giggles.

'Nor me,' all the others piped in.

'Good grief, I'm completely dry and darling, well, actually all of you, you look so much younger and healthier,' Sir Harry said, smiling.

They all turned to see rows and rows of the purest, whitest gowns glistening in the pale light and, beside them, white slip-on shoes.

'Quickly, everyone, put these on, and leave all your old clothes next to the pool,' Jonny said while pulling the purest and whitest gown around him and standing in the new shoes, which fit like a glove.

'Mmmmmmmmmm, that feels so nice, like being cocooned in a soft cloud,' Jonny added. Soon, everyone was dressed in the purest, whitest gowns and slip-ons.

'Are you all ready? Legend, Legion, are you ready?'

'Yes,' everybody replied.

Without warning, they were all lifted into the air by some kind of beam, high into the centre of this giant spaceship.

'Come with us, Nanny Noo, please, please, come with us,' Lady Kathleen urged as they all floated skywards.

'What about the house?' Nanny Noo asked.

'Oh, it will still be here when we come back,' Jonny replied, adding, 'It's being rebuilt stone by stone right now, and if you don't believe me, I will show you before we go.'

'You never told us where we were going, old chap,' Sir Harry asked.

'Pashoo,' everybody replied, 'we're all going to Pashoo.'

'Wow, that is exciting, old chap, but where on earth is Pashoo?'

'Outer space, old boy, outer space,' Sir Ranulf replied, smiling. Suddenly, they all found themselves in a vast circular room, bathed with the gentlest hues. There were several huge sofas made from what looked like floating clouds. They all stood in stunned silence.

'Hello Jonny, welcome to the Arc.'

'PAL, hello PAL,' Jonny shouted at the top of his voice.

'Hello Jonny, hello Jonny's family, hello Legend and Legion, hello Nanny Noo, hello Stan. Welcome to your new home. Now, if you would all like to look downwards.'

Without a moment's hesitation, everybody peered to the floor, which, like the floor of the Silver Flying Arrow Spaceship, suddenly became invisible. Far below was their old home, rebuilt exactly as it was with new occupants.

'Good grief, who on earth is that?' Sir Ranulf asked.

'You,' PAL replied.

'Me?'

'Yes, it's you.'

'But that's impossible because I'm up here, in this spaceship.'

'Well, it appears you are in both places; look, you're waving to yourself,' Lady Kathleen said, laughing.

'Oh, and there's me,' Nanny Carole said, jumping up and down with excitement.

'I don't understand, I don't understand this at all,' Professor Ziad said as he watched himself pulling up outside the house in his old mini, adding, 'God, don't I look old.'

'Well, where am I then?' Philomena Flatulent Fudge-Bucket asked.

'At the Doctors, probably, sorting out your haemorrhoids,' Professor Ziad laughed.

'Not sure I want to return to being that chunky, plump, parping woman,' Philomena said mournfully.

'Yes, I tend to agree with that,' Professor Ziad said, looking at the radiant beauty beside him.

'We all look so young and healthy. What was that pool under your house, Ranulf?' Sir Harry asked.

'The Elixir of Life, old boy; you, I, all of us, are now cured of all illnesses,' Sir Ranulf replied.

'So, who exactly are those people down there?' Lady Bunty asked meekly.

'They are what we know as holograms,' Jonny replied, adding, 'just to make sure it all looks normal when it's far from normal.'

'Well, don't you have one, a hologranny then?' Lady Bunty asked.

'Hologram, Bunty, not a hologranny, and yes, there is one of us, but as we know, evil is coming, and when it arrives, it will think we're all there when, in fact, we won't be; we will be here. Well, not here exactly; we will be a few million light-years away...'

'...I knew I had something to tell you,' Sir Harry Pinner blurted out, 'God, how could I forget? Oh, I know, huge spaceship above your home and bottomless pool in the cellar.'

'Yes, well, what did you forget to tell us, old chap?'

'The news, on the radio, as we were driving back from Dover. NASA reckoned three thunderous explosions in space, and the Vatican also said something about an infant child being born.'

'Is that it, nothing else? I mean, about the infant child?' Jonny asked, sounding worried.

'Yes, sorry old boy, they don't know what the three explosions were or what caused...'

'I do,' Jonny whispered, cutting Sir Harry off mid-sentence.

'...them. What do you mean, you do?'

'I do, as in I know what these things are.'

'You do?'

'I do.'

'Well, well, old boy, spill the beans.'

'The three huge explosions were two supermassive black holes...' Jonny stopped momentarily, thinking back to another conversation he had with PAL about supermassive black holes.

'Yes, supermassive black holes,' Sir Harry urged.

'Sorry, got sidetracked by Sloppy Botty's supermassive black hole,' Jonny replied, giggling.

'Soppy Dotty! Who is Soppy Dotty, a mad relative?'

'No, no, no, sorry, where was I? Oh yeah, two supermassive black holes have collided in deep space, and the noise they heard is a new galaxy being formed.'

'Oh, is that all? Just for a moment, I was getting worried,' Lady Kathleen laughed.

'We should be because the third noise...' Jonny paused for a moment, wondering if he should tell the unexpected audience what was coming out of the two exploding supermassive black holes. '...is what's coming from the two exploding supermassive black holes.'

'Ok, Jonny, you have us all scared now,' Nanny Carole said, grabbing Charlie's hand.

'Hell is.'

'But I thought we had defeated them?' Nanny Noo said, making Lady Bunty and Sir Harry shriek with fear.

'Yes, we did, but I knew something wasn't right when the Devil sent his daughter Deadsheda, who was a bit wet and was easily killed by custard. I am unsure if what's coming next will be so easy to destroy.'

'She killed me,' Nanny Noo growled.

'What, you're dead?' Lady Bunty said in astonishment before passing out.

'Why do you think we are in the giant spaceship called the Arc then?' Jonny replied.

'No idea, old boy,' Sir Harry replied, completely ignoring his wife, who was lying flat on what looked like a floating cloud.

'To save Jonny and us,' Sir Ranulf replied.

'What about the rest of humanity?'

'Well, the Devil will sell to the stupid to amass his armies...'

'Where does the Devil keep his armies?' Legion butted in.

'We don't know, Legend, where does the Devil keep his armies?' everybody replied.

'Up his sleevies,' Legend replied, laughing.

'Oh yes, very droll, very funny, Legion,' Jonny replied.

'Ahem,' PAL butted in. 'I think it's time to leave.'

Suddenly, everybody stopped laughing and looked at each other. Realising what was happening snapped them out of their stupidity and childishness. They were about to leave Earth, unsure when or if they would return.

'I don't want to leave,' wailed Lady Bunty.

'No, nor do I,' said Nanny Carole.

'Or me,' Charlie said, shaking.

'You can all stay if you want; you all know this, but Jonny can't unless you want the Devil and his evil sidekicks to kill him. Jonny gave you all a choice. If you want to stay and return to your normal, uninteresting lives, just put your hands up, and you can return in seconds. Your choice, your decision,' PAL said, justifiably angry.

Lady Bunty slowly raised her hand; then Nanny Carole and Charlie did.

'Anyone else want to stay?' Jonny asked.

Lady Kathleen then slowly raised her hand.

'Oh no, darling, not you as well?' Sir Ranulf whined.

'Because, because, I am frightened.'

'We're all frightened,' Professor Ziad whispered as his wife raised her hand.

'We're from Earth, Jonny; this is our home, not Pashoo. Here is where our home is, not billions of miles away,' Lady Kathleen said as she gently stroked Jonny's face.

'Anyone else wants to go back?' Jonny asked sullenly.

'I have a girlfriend that I want to marry and a job that I love,' PC Floppy said, raising his hand.

'Lady Taylor, what about you?'

'No. I'm not going back to that Wacky Shacky. I have already lost my mind once, lost my silly husband, and I don't ever intend to lose Isobel.'

'So that leaves Dad, Sir Harry, and Professor Ziad. Are you sure you want to come, Professor? I mean, you don't have to,' Jonny asked.

'I must admit to being torn between the two: my work here, my wife, and our simple life. It's not an easy choice, and I don't know what to do,' the Professor sighed.

'Then stay. I don't want anyone to come if they don't want to,' Jonny said, smiling. 'But leave the gowns and the rather snazzy slippers.'

'Ok, so that leaves Mother Mary, Dad, Harry, Mrs Taylor, and Isobel. Is that it?' Jonny said quite forlornly.

'I don't want to go.' Jonny spun around to see Isobel with her hand in the air.

'What, no, not you, Isobel, please, no Isobel.'

'If Isobel's not going, then nor am I. I am cured, so I have no fear of returning.'

'I can't go either, Jonny,' Sir Ranulf sighed, 'I can't leave your mother, really I cannot.'

'So that just leaves Mary, Legend, and Legion?' Jonny asked in absolute exasperation.

'Yes, Jonny,' Sir Ranulf replied as he put his massive arms around his trembling son's body.

'You came here alone, Jonny. Now you must return alone,' Lady Kathleen said with tears streaming down her face. Jonny turned to see both Lady Kathleen and his birth mother crying.

'You're not coming either, are you?'

'No, my son, I cannot,' Mary replied. Jonny sat down on the sofa cloud, placed his head deep into his hands, and openly wept. Legion and Legend walked over and sat close, right next to him.

'We will take care of the Elixir, and we will wait for you, no matter how long you take,' whispered a tearful Sir Ranulf. Suddenly, and without warning, his entire family just vanished out of view, leaving Jonny no time to reply or react.

'Jonny,' Legend whispered, 'we need to talk. PAL, move the Arc into outer space where we can be alone. There are too many people gathering outside.'

'We are in outer space,' PAL said quietly, 'no one can bother us here.'

'Now, where was I? Oh yes, you have been asked to return because your star parents don't think you are ready to fight yet another battle. What do you think?'

'It's strange. I have learnt the wisdom from all the wisest teachers in the universe by living on the nine orbiting planets of Pashoo: Bodha (knowledge), Boddhi (enlightenment), Suddha (pure), Jala (water), Turya (deep sleep), Krodha (anger), Yajna (sacrifice), Mithya (false/unreal), and Tattvam (reality).

I have fought, beaten, and imprisoned the Gnud Repeek. I have fought and beaten Deadsheda and those cackling witches, DanceswithDeath. I have fought, beaten, and destroyed the Ghost Riders of Firestorm. Then I met, ate with, and incarcerated those insidious weirdos, the Icelandic Yule Lads. I befriended

Sally the Lathfliothsorthmurnnth and Mary the Mincing Sea Monster, also known as The Aspidoceleon. I have travelled through and around the universe to find the Shard of Pure Light, the Thirteen Runes, 100 Phials, the Golden Globe, and the Bone Ring. I have also met the hologram Queen of Iceland and then met the real Queen of Iceland, who gave me, not anyone else, the rose petal of Amaranta. Then I got Isobel's tear, a hair from StumpGrinding, which was like a tree trunk, and cleaned the revolting wax and grunge from his cave-like ears. I have collected and cut myself on the Shark's Tooth, then recited the Lord's Prayer to create the Elixir of Life and freed Cosmos.'

'Yeah, Jonny, you're right; you have done incredible things for a kid from a children's home. There is no doubting that,' Legion said gently.

'And, and I cured Sloppy Botty's parping bottom. I am proud of that one, especially that one. Then what about saving my Dad and Harry from the Mad Mud Monkeys from Drak Gob and healing Fat Wallet, Plug and Pillock,' Jonny said excitedly as if his entire future depended on what he had so heroically achieved and all while wearing his shorts.

'Plus, your school won its first-ever football game,' Legend added.

'Yeah, and then I gave the headmaster, the headmistress, and that thick footballer, Floppy Leg.'

'You certainly did, Jonny, you certainly did, Jonny,' Legion said proudly.

'So, tell me again, Legend, why should I run away like a scared little boy?' Legend asked.

Suddenly, a flash of brilliant white light temporarily blinded Jonny, Legend, and Legion.

'Jonny, I am Spirit, your father. If you return to Pashoo, you will become immortal and live forever, but if you stay on earth, you will become human. The evil coming to earth is too strong for you, Jonny and the evil that has just been born will forever try to harm you. I have spoken at length with the nine elders, and we all agree on one thing: for your safety, you must return home.'

Jonny looked up from his cloud sofa, still unable to see correctly, still blinded by the light, but soon his vision returned to see the beautiful spectre of his father standing, dressed from head to toe in the most beautiful white gown, which was full of the stars of Pashoo.

'Father, I am not scared of dying, and I am not scared of living. However, I am scared of being alone.'

'Wise words, my son, wise words.'

'Father, together, we have an incredible bond and incredible strength. My new family have shown me what true love can do. It makes you want to care, love, and protect them all as they have all cared, loved, and protected me. Why can't we all stand together against the forthcoming evil rather than be separated by time and space? Why can't the good people of the earth beat the evil that's been born and the evil that now speeds towards us? Why, Father, why?'

'Nerrac, you must now speak,' Spirit ordered.

'Spirit, the boy is right. Only together as one can we defeat the evil that comes and the evil that's been born,' Nerrac replied in a deep voice that sounded like thunder. His magnificent mane shone with the stars of Pashoo. Jonny suddenly felt very small and feeble as he sat open-mouthed, staring at his Star Father and the fearsome size and unbelievable strength of Nerrac.

'Excuse me,' Jonny asked timidly, 'but does this yet-to-be-born evil child have a name?'

'Not as far as we are aware, but the Vatican suggests the number eight, though I have no idea why,' Spirit replied.

Jonny drew an imaginary figure eight in the air with his finger and then whispered, 'Perhaps it's an initial, like a B.'

'Balaam,' Spirit, Nerrac, and Jonny shouted at once.

'Perhaps all the evil ever known and has ever been is being reborn and then hiding behind the names of famous people, perhaps ones with the letter B in their names,' Jonny said almost silently.

'Or more likely the initials of their last name,' Nerrac replied. Suddenly and without warning, Jonny's entire family and friends reappeared as Nerrac disappeared and returned to being Legion and Legend, and Spirit vanished into thin air. The spaceship returned to Earth, hovering above the newly rebuilt Trevena.

'Jonny, have you decided to stay with us or return to Pashoo?' Sir Ranulf asked.

'Yes, Father, I have.'

'So, what decision have you made?' Lady Kathleen asked, hoping that he would stay.

'I will tell you tomorrow,' Jonny replied, smiling while gently drifting to sleep on the sofa cloud.

Jonny slept soundly for hours and hours with his two best friends in the world snuggled up next to him. Jonny dreamt about all the adventures he had since he arrived from his orphanage with nothing but a pair of old leather boots, with the laces still untied, his battered old suitcase with all his meagre possessions placed carefully inside, and most importantly, his beaten-up but much-loved old teddy bear, Pod.

Jonny suddenly woke with a jolt and, through sleep-filled eyes, looked around.

'Where am I, Legion, Legend, where am I?????'

The End